Etta

ANGEL TALES

ANGEL TALES

FROM *NEW YORK TIMES* BESTSELLING AUTHOR

CATHERINE LANIGAN

PLAIN SIGHT PUBLISHING
AN IMPRINT OF CEDAR FORT, INC.
SPRINGVILLE, UTAH

ISBN 13: 978-1-59955-991-9

Published by Plain Sight Publishing, an imprint of Cedar Fort, Inc.
2373 W. 700 S., Springville, UT, 84663
Distributed by Cedar Fort, Inc., www.cedarfort.com

LIBRARY OF CONGRESS CATALOGING-IN-PUBLICATION DATA

Lanigan, Catherine, author.
  Angel tales / Catherine Lanigan.
    pages cm
  ISBN 978-1-59955-991-9
  1. Angels--Fiction. I. Title.

  PS3562.A53A84 2011
  813'.54--dc23

2011043652

Cover design by Angela D. Olsen
Cover design © 2012 by Lyle Mortimer
Edited and typeset by Kelley Konzak

Printed in the United States of America

10 9 8 7 6 5 4 3 2 1

Printed on acid-free paper

THIS BOOK is dedicated to the angels on the other side who believe in me and my God-given talent. My father, Frank Lanigan; My mother, Dorothy Lanigan; my sister, Nancy Lanigan Porter; my uncles, Jack and Dick Manning; and my grandparents, Ethel and C.F. Manning and Grace and Ed Lanigan.

OTHER BOOKS BY CATHERINE LANIGAN

Seduced

Web of Deceit

Admit Desire

Promise Made

Bound by Love

Christmas Star

Writing the Great American Romance Novel

Wings of Destiny

Evolving Woman

CONTENTS

INTRODUCTION

T HIS BOOK HAS BEEN INSPIRED BY YOU, MY READERS. I have conducted dozens of radio interviews regarding angels and their intervention into human life, and the result has been a plethora of emails and letters from those of you who listened with both your ears and your hearts. I've been happily stunned at the extent of your amazing experiences. Once again, I was profoundly affected in both my heart and my soul at how wondrous God truly is. He never abandons us and is continually sending his angels and messengers to protect us, guide us, talk to us, and show themselves to us.

There are some who believe that this planet is on a collision course to disaster and that is the reason the angels are showing up more now than ever before.

I'm not so sure about this.

Because we live in a high-tech world, with the Internet and reality television programs, many of us are speaking out now about events we have never dared to share with even the closest of friends. Many of us are afraid of being labeled as "crazy" or "insane." This is a justifiable concern. The Internet phenomenon of bloggers who can and do say anything they want and can condemn anyone who doesn't think just like they do makes us all potential targets of ridicule and even of being ostracized. What is worse, the press, political poll takers, and marketing experts are listening to bloggers and not taking the time to investigate allegations and statements. Our era of "instant journalism" reminds me of the scandal of "yellow journalism" that plagued our nation in the 1880s. Back then, once we'd had enough false reporting, the media endeavored to regulate itself.

Translate that past and the current threat to be labeled a "kook" or a "nut case" by anyone who doesn't believe exactly the same way as the critic, and it is even more admirable that so many of you have stepped forward in this manner.

In the section in this book concerning near-death experiences, there are several stories that both validate the existence of heaven and illuminate facets of the next life that you might not have heard anywhere else.

It is vital to the mission of this book to tell the stories of our "experiencers" in as close to their own words as possible. I endeavored to simply be the journalist in this book. During my father's last days on earth, when he was quite coherent and speaking to me about the life he was living "between the worlds," he told me that the "beings of light" were telling him that my new divine mission was to "chronicle stories about angels and life on the other side." In this book, *Angel Tales*, my endeavor is to keep my promise not only to my father but also to the angels who gave me this directive.

This collection of stories, then, bears a great responsibility to those who have participated in its creation. These people have reached into their memories and their pasts to help light the way for others who are seeking help, courage, and strength in their time of need.

To be human is to have failings. To be frail. Few of us can make it all the way from the cradle to the grave without, at some time, dropping to our knees and asking the great Unknown Void, "What is the meaning of my life?" Even those with no spiritual beliefs believe in something, whether it is "science" or the "theory of chaos." We all have to have something, some place to go, to hang our hats on hope.

It is my purpose to present to you these real stories for you to analyze, connect with, accept, or reject. In no way do I make a judgment about what others have seen or heard. To the best of my ability, I have not embellished or distorted the facts of what took place. These incidents are too vital to our lives. I feel it is important to write the words just as each angel spoke them in order for us to piece together this spiritual puzzle that baffles most of us even though, frankly, it shouldn't.

To have faith is to believe what we can't see.

There are many, sometimes too many, times in our lives when, though we have been filled with faith and are faithful, we falter. We become deeply troubled and incredibly afraid, and our faith comes up wanting.

This book is for those times.

These stories are meant to give hope and a sense of peace when you need it most. These stories are from people who are just like you. They were in trouble, and they were helped by a divine intercession.

What is most important for you, our new readers, to know is that these people were in trouble, but they listened for the angels. They were open to the angels. When an angel showed up, they didn't just rationalize the experience. They accepted that God was working in their lives like he always does.

Therefore, it is important for you to keep your ears open to hear and your eyes open to see. Your miracle is right in front of you. Accept it. Accept God's abundance in your life, every day of your life.

SECTION ONE

Angelic Visitations

ANGELIC VISITATIONS

THE STORIES IN THIS SECTION PERTAIN TO THOSE VISITA-
tions that occur while a person is awake. These occurrences
involve the angel appearing in human form only. If an onlooker
were to witness a true "visitation," there would be nothing out
of the human realm of experience to report. These angels do not
have wings. They are dressed in whatever the current fashion or
mode of dress is for the country and culture in which they mani-
fest themselves. They speak in the known dialect and language of
that country or tribe. Their very existence at the moment of their
visitation is purposely fashioned so as not to bring attention to
themselves. They are about the work.

These stories are not "apparitions" in which the angel appears
to a person and, other than speaking to the person or giving a
message, the angel does not actually interact with the person or
perform any kind of physical work or perform physical healing.

I would like to take a moment to explain "apparitions."

Most of us have heard of these kinds of stories in which the
angel, resplendent in white gowns and with enormous wings,
appears to a holy person, saint, or prophet. There are many of this
kind of angel story in the Bible. For the most part, we feel disconnected with those ancient times when people seemed to have a
better shot at being visited by an angel than we do in contempo-
rary times. Or did they?

About fifteen years ago, I met a woman, Kathy Gillian (not

her real name), in Houston, Texas. At the time, she was a fairly prominent psychic in Houston. She worked at a day spa not far from where I worked in the pool industry. Kathy had been interviewed by the leading local newspapers and had been on several television shows. Today, that doesn't seem all that odd, especially considering the popularity of the programs "Medium" and "The Pet Psychic" that have inundated our cable and networks.

I had gone to Kathy's apartment to consult about a charity event we were both hosting. I asked her if she had ever seen an angel. She told me that when she was only four or five years old, she had been playing in her bedroom. She saw a bright light, and when she looked up from her dolls, the walls and ceiling of her room had simply disappeared. It was as if dense matter had transformed to ethereal light and energy. And there with her was an angel. The angel was very tall, blond, and blue eyed, and it wore white robes and a white gown. It had a gold rope belt around its waist. Kathy said she couldn't tell if the angel was male or female, because it felt like both. (This kind of report is why I always refer to this kind of angel as androgynous.)

She was not ill at the time. She was not in any danger at all. The angel had come to tell her that she was not alone and would never be alone. She was to understand that God loved her and that her life would be a very special one. She would always "see" things that other people did not. She was to have patience with other humans who could not "see" nor understand what Kathy would see.

Once Kathy was an adult, she was revisited by her angel only a handful of times, but she did feel that the angel spoke to her and through her each time she was giving guidance to one of her clients. She never felt disconnected from her angel, and it was a constant source of comfort, hope, and love.

As simple as this apparition story is, it has stayed with me all these years.

Kathy had never been in danger of her life when she saw her angel.

In this "angelic visitations" section, the stories are true interactions with angels. Most times when this type of interaction takes place, the humans are either in danger of their lives or are in such great despair and hopelessness that angelic intervention is necessary.

From the stories submitted to me, I have established criteria for this kind of angelic visitation.

- The angel, in human form, appears seemingly out of nowhere.
- The angel is a total stranger.
- The angel vanishes into thin air moments after the "lifesaving" moment or the danger has passed or, at the very least, is never heard from or seen again, as if that person didn't exist.

As fantastic and strange as some of these stories may sound, I believe that in addition to the obvious need for the angel's appearance and interaction with the human in question during times of danger or need, these wonderful situations also make us aware that angels truly do live.

LIGHTNING BOLT ANGEL

AUTHOR'S NOTE: This story was submitted to me by Reverend Dr. Richard Stewart, who is the author of "Angel on the Land Rover," which also appears in this collection. My very deep thanks to Dr. Steward for sharing his story, but after reading the following story, I certainly hope there are no more such dramatic experiences from him again!

July 13, 2006

I JUST HAD A LIFESAVING EVENT WITH AN ANGEL ONCE again. This time I was the recipient of an angel's touch.

A week ago, Tuesday, July 4, 2006, I was at a friend's house for a late supper snack. I was preparing to leave around ten thirty at night.

A fast-moving and vicious thunderstorm blew in. The lightning was frequent and very dangerous. The thunder was very loud. Loud enough to shake and rattle homes.

The storm took thirty minutes to pass. When I thought the storm was passed enough to go out to my car about one hundred yards down the street, I said good night to my friend.

I shook my buddy's hand, and he disappeared down the cellar steps.

I opened the front door and began to step out.

Suddenly, I felt a strong tug on the collar of my T-shirt. It pulled me back inside the house. I almost fell over backwards, the tug was so strong.

I regained my composure once inside the door. I turned around to see who was there and found no one.

"Okay. That was weird," I said to myself.

I looked out the front door. Suddenly, a last blast of lightning

10

struck the power and phone lines directly across the street, setting off every fire alarm and smoke alarm in every condominium in the community my friend lives in.

Immediately following the lightning was a blast of thunder so loud that it shattered numerous closed windows in a number of condos.

The thunder was so loud and the percussion so strong that it knocked me over backward, sending me to my rear end and then over my head!

My buddy, James, looked back up the cellar stairs and asked, "Are you okay?"

"Yes."

"Thank God."

"Precisely," I said. "I have never experienced a blast of lightning and thunder that would send me over backward."

I knew then and I know now that if it had not been for that "invisible hand" grabbing me by the shirt collar, I would have been struck by lightning.

TAILSPIN ANGEL

AUTHOR'S NOTE: This is a wonderful story from Patricia Moore-Donley. So many of us are involved in potentially deadly car accidents and incidents. Too many times everything happens so fast that it is difficult for us to remember precisely what happened. Certainly sometimes, it's even impossible to explain these lost details to the highway patrolman or policeman who keeps asking us how it is that we were able to live through such bizarre circumstances.

In our modern existence on this earth at the current time, mankind is no longer battling dinosaurs and saber-toothed tigers. Thus, our daily lives are not particularly riddled with life-threatening situations. However, for each and every one of us who gets behind the wheel of a car and must battle the daily commute on our nation's freeways and highways, there is almost always a conscious or subconscious sigh of relief once we get to our final destination and we realize that, once again, we made it alive.

Each time I read one of these stories about the near misses that my friends, family, and new email and Facebook acquaintances have experienced, I am filled with wonder and awe at just how busy the angels must be during rush hour. As I've always said, "For most of us, it takes several angelic interventions on a daily basis to keep us safe."

IT WAS IN THE 1970S WHEN PATRICIA BOUGHT HER FIRST car. It was a purple AMC Gremlin, and she was very proud of it. For anyone who knows anything about cars, this was a small car with a small engine. Even at the time, it was not considered the safest car on the road.

It was a frigid winter evening when Patricia drove her boyfriend to his home and then started on her way back to Cincinnati. Once she got to the freeway, the snow was coming down very hard. She had the windshield wipers going, and she was hunched over the steering wheel trying to see the cars ahead of her. Fortunately, the traffic was light, but she had to make her way slowly.

She got to the section of I-75 South that was surrounded by a twenty-five-foot tall concrete wall that was near the city called Lockland. She was in the fast lane, going about thirty-five miles per hour, when her car suddenly started to skid. It started spinning in circles, going around and around. She ended up facing the wrong way in the slow lane with an oncoming semitruck barreling down on her.

Patricia screamed and didn't know what to do. The truck was only about one hundred feet from her. From her vantage point, she could see the shocked and frightened look on the truck driver's face as he braced for the inevitable impact.

At that moment, she believed that they were both about to die.

Patricia braced for the impact. She shut her eyes and screamed out loud, "Oh, God! Get me out of this!"

At this instant, Patricia felt her leg being lifted off the brake pedal. Then her foot smashed down on the accelerator pedal. Suddenly the car was spinning again. Only one spin.

Patricia found herself in the emergency lane facing southbound again. At that precise moment, the semi went careening past her. Miraculously, the impact had been avoided without a second to spare.

Patricia shouted, "Thank you!"

Patricia was well aware that another force was responsible for lifting her leg off the brake and putting her foot on the accelerator. At the time, she had been too frozen with fear to react to the situation. There had been no thought in her head about what to do. All she thought about was the fact that she was going to die.

Afterward, she was shaking as she took hold of the steering wheel once again and made her way home. However, Patricia was incredibly thankful because she knew that her life had just been saved by some divine intervention. All the way home that night she continued to thank God and her angels for saving her life once again.

PILOT ANGEL TO THE RESCUE

AUTHOR'S NOTE: What follows here are two stories of angelic intervention in one man's life.

IN THE LATE 1950S, LEO MOSELEY AND HIS FRIEND WERE challenged to a race in his friend's new Oldsmobile 88. Because his friend had recently consumed several beers and Leo had not been drinking, they decided that Leo should drive.

They met their challenger on an uncompleted interstate highway not far from their city. It was dark, and there were no street lamps to light the area. They had to rely on headlights from their cars and those of a few friends who were their cheering section.

They revved their engines, each trying to outdo the other with a display of noisy, intended intimidation. A friend dropped a bandanna, and the race was on.

The cars had raced only about a half a mile when Leo's challenger began blowing his horn. Suddenly, the challenger dropped back. Leo was going over one hundred miles per hour as he glanced in the rearview mirror to see his challenger frantically waving at him and now dropping very far behind.

Leo looked straight ahead, and in his headlights he could see a large wooden barrier with huge red stripes painted across it. Behind the barrier were two very large oak trees. Leo knew he was going to crash into the barrier and that the car would continue careening into the two oak trees.

"I'm going to die!"

Leo started to cover his face with his hands so as not to see the collision.

At that very second, there was a flash of blinding light, and everything came to a standstill.

Miraculously, the impact never came. There was no

thunderous, crashing sound. No twisted metal. No pain to Leo and no agonizing screams from his friend in the passenger seat.

Leo sat there completely amazed that they had not crashed.

He got out of the car, wobbly but alive. As he looked around, he realized that the car was sitting facing in the opposite direction with the motor still idling. To his astonishment, the back bumper was only several inches from the barrier.

His friend got out of the car and stared at Leo, neither of them saying a word.

Within moments, the challenger drove up to Leo and his friend. He got out of the car and said, "I can't believe you guys are alive."

"Neither can we," Leo said.

"There is no way you could stop that car in time to avoid a crash. That's some of the best driving I've ever seen. How did you do it?"

"I don't know," Leo said.

The next day Leo and his friend got together. They discussed everything that they remembered and both their stories were exactly the same.

"We shouldn't be alive, Leo," his friend said to him.

"It had to be divine intervention," Leo said. "I will never forget that flash of light."

"It was an angel, if you ask me," his friend said.

"I think you're right. I hope he sticks around just in case I need him again," Leo said.

Several years later, Leo was to encounter an angel in another life-threatening situation.

In the early 1960s, Leo was a twenty-two-year-old military fighter pilot. He was involved in a training flight in which he was practicing dissimilar combat maneuvering. In this flight, two different types of aircraft practiced their tactics against one another. This practice had taken place over an hour or so.

Leo was returning back to the air base when he experienced an engine flameout. The engines had completely stopped running. Leo tried an in-flight air restart. But the restart failed. Suddenly, Leo lost control of the aircraft. He was going down.

He tried to eject out of the cockpit, but the ejection seat would not fire because the safety pin had not been removed. Thinking fast, Leo blew the canopy off the aircraft and continued going through the emergency procedures. He tried manually to bail out, but due to the forces involved, he was pinned to the seat and could not move.

He looked out through the top of the aircraft and saw the ground rushing up toward him. His mind raced with a thousand thoughts as he went speeding toward the earth. He continued struggling with the aircraft, trying to recover his altitude.

For the second time, he looked up, and now he saw a large tree looming in front of him. At this moment, Leo was convinced he was going to die.

"My God!" he screamed.

At that very instant, and for the second time in his young life, he saw a blinding flash of light. Everything in his world seemed to come to a standstill.

By this time, the aircraft should have impacted with the earth. Instead, Leo went flying about fifty feet above the trees, at wing's level, and the engines were running smoothly.

There was no other damage than the loss of the canopy. All the military personnel and crew on the ground commented how they could not believe what had happened. They knew, just as did Leo, that he should've crashed.

They also knew that something or someone had saved Leo.

Today, Leo states that his philosophy of life has changed drastically and that now he is much more spiritual. He states, "I also know that we are much more than our bodies. Over the years, when in physical danger and during periods of emotional stress, I can feel the presence of a loving force surrounding me, and on several occasions have heard a very loving, kind voice tell me, 'All is well. Do not be concerned.'"

Potawatomi Portal

AUTHOR'S NOTE: This story was sent to me by Susan Kay Menkes Simonson with the blessing of her husband Bruce Simonson, both of whom I knew growing up in La Porte, Indiana.

Suzi, Bruce, and I are from a small town. Bruce was two years ahead of me in school, but we attended St. Peter Catholic Grade School together. There were nine children in the Simonson family, so each of my brothers and my sister had a Simonson child in their respective classes. We all knew the Rumelys, whose story, "A Phone Call from Fran," was related in *Divine Nudges: Tales of Angelic Intervention.*

Suzi's parents were also friends of my mother and father, and they all traveled to Bermuda together in 1969. They were all involved in the community, church, and area politics together. We grew up at a time in America when everyone chipped in together to build our towns and cities. We all knew our neighbors. We didn't lock our doors and we didn't ask questions if someone called and said, "I need you." We all couldn't wait to help someone out. There were very few people in my past who thought about what they would get out of giving aid or time or sweat to help their community or their friends. That's what I love about going home to my hometown. There's still a heart there, and it's beating quite soundly.

True, there are many communities much like my hometown today, but we live in a world where terrorists are a real threat to our lives, and we must be on guard and be watchful perhaps more than any other time in our history. I believe this is also why we are hearing more and more about angel visitations. We are being protected.

I'm explaining all this because Suzi was one of our "model" citizens in La Porte during the years I knew her in high school. She was one of the kids everyone looked up to and wanted to emulate. She graduated with honors from high school, went on to receive "High Scholastic Achievement Awards" from the Indiana

University Foundation, and was a member of Phi Beta Kappa in 1969. From 1988–89 she was listed in "Notable 2000 American Distinguished Women," and in 1989–90, Suzi was listed in International Leaders in Achievement.

Most of her life, Suzi has worked in bilingual education, social services, and presently as clinical care coordinator, clinical resource management. Her résumé is nine pages long, listing all her achievements, awards, honoraria, and publications. She is an accomplished woman, yet she has taken the time to share her experiences with us.

It had been decades since I was in touch with Suzi or Bruce. However, recently they had read my last book, *Divine Nudges: Tales of Angelic Intervention,* and were specifically attracted to one story in particular, "Hometown Halloween." Suzi related to me that not only was she close and dear friends to two of the Zimmerman girls, Ginna and Kathy, she had also been a visitor many times to the Zimmerman house. She also stated that she had heard the story about the incident with the newel post and the belt.

Suzi told me that she can confirm one time following Kathy and Ginna up the stairs in the house and that she "felt someone was following" her. Of course, once she turned around, there was no one there. She commented to the girls about her perceptions.

They replied, "Oh, that's usual."

For me, to have Suzi's validation of a story that happened decades ago in my memory and my ninety-one-year-old mother's memory, is a blessing.

I was doubly excited and intrigued when I received a very large package of information from Suzi. Several stories are included in the wealthy spiritual life that Suzi has lived. In this package, Suzi included photocopied research and reports to back up the dreams, waking memories, out-of-body experiences, spiritual visitations, and manifestations she has encountered since her early childhood. She sent photographs to validate her stories that were, frankly, astonishing.

I am honored to be working with Suzi and Bruce to bring these experiences to light and to share them with you, our readers. The following is from Suzi.

M Y SPIRITUAL RECOLLECTIONS BEGAN AT APPROXI-mately the age of five.

At that time, my father took me to a meeting with Louis Moe at the Moe cottages in Galena Township near Rolling Prairie. The eighty acres of land were part of the original Potawatomi Indian reservation until they (the Indians) were relocated in about 1867 to Oklahoma and Kansas. The property includes woods, a creek, and an Indian burial ground.

While Dad met with Mr. Moe, I went down the hill toward the creek to explore. It was a beautiful area, overgrown with grasses and vines and trees. Just the way the sunlight sifted through the trees to·dapple the ground with puddles of golden light seemed magical.

While I was standing at the creek watching the water trickle over tree roots and rocks, I looked up and saw several white, willowy spirits floating in the air.

They told me that they were Potawatomi Indians and that they weren't really dead; they were still there.

They told me not to tell the grown-ups because they wouldn't believe me.

I watched them float for quite a bit of time. The experience was very real. So real that I haven't forgotten it.

I never did tell anyone about my experience. It wasn't until after Bruce and I were married that I related the story to him.

Dad bought that property, and I spent all my childhood and young adult summers there. I loved the area and picked wildflowers and mushrooms, which were abundant. I waded in the creek and dug in the Indian burial ground.

One day while I was playing in the woods, I saw a round, lighted area that appeared to be suspended between the trees. The light was shimmering. I knew it wasn't sunlight like I'd seen every day in the woods for weeks and months. This was different.

I stood there, transfixed by the white light. Then I felt as if I were melting into the light.

I did not receive any communication from spirits or Indian spirits or angels. I simply remember being enveloped by this wonderful, peaceful, white and yellow light.

Because of this profound experience and the earlier one of meeting the Potawatomi Indian spirits when I was five years old, I have gone to some lengths in my life to find an explanation.

In 1988 I participated in an art therapy workshop. The artist, Margaret Carpenter, told us that "every picture tells a story." She asked us to draw three pictures. The first was of our most special place.

Of course, my special place was that spot by the creek in the woods near Rolling Prairie, Indiana.

When I drew my self-portrait drawing, as crude as my own artist's hand was, I was astonished to see what I had actually depicted. I drew a creek and green grass and a few sparse trees. However, I couldn't find enough yellow pencils to color the entire sheet of paper with all the yellow light I had experienced. I wore that yellow pencil to a nub!

Interestingly, when Margaret and I looked at the figure that was supposed to be me, I was suspended in the air. I had no feet, barely any legs. My arms were stretched out to my sides, and they weren't arms at all, but wings! They were very similar to angel's wings.

Above me was a shower of stronger light. The glowing light all around me was pure gold. I was facing the light as it was coming toward me.

Even in my most perfectly remembered memories, I had not given these attributes to my experience. I did not remember feeling like an angel, seeing an angel, or becoming an angel. However, when I allowed my mind to take over this project and to put the real truth down on paper, I believe what I drew was what actually happened to me. When I look at my drawing, I know I'm looking at the truth.

In my endeavor to continue seeking the truth about my experience, no matter where that road would take me, I continued to ask questions, research other people's encounters with angels and spirits, and pay attention to my dreams.

I don't remember every dream I've ever had. None of us do. However, there are some dreams that seem so real that I believe they are real.

After Bruce and I were married, I dreamed that the two of us lived at "the farm" with our parents. We lived in a square house made of sticks covered with deerskin. I was Bruce's older sister.

Armed soldiers arrived one day to relocate us.

Bruce and I ran into the creek in the woods to escape. Bruce was in front of me as the soldiers chased us.

I heard a loud CRACK! And then I felt something hit me in the back. I fell face forward into the creek. I screamed at Bruce to keep running, and he escaped.

I had been shot in the back and died in the creek.

Not long after I attended Margaret Carpenter's workshop and drew my drawing of my encounter with the light, she introduced Bruce and I to a friend of hers who was a psychic, Angie Hanson. Bruce and I told Angie nothing about ourselves in this life or any other life.

Astonishingly, she immediately told us that we had been brother and sister in a previous life and that I had been eight years older than Bruce. This was precisely the age difference I determined we were in the dream I have just related.

She then told me that I had always been a "brown person" in my previous lives and that this was my first time as a Caucasian.

Another interesting note is that in 1966 at Indiana University, I commissioned a charcoal portrait of myself to be made as a gift for my parents. They never liked that portrait. They said that it didn't look like me. Truthfully, I resembled the Indian girl in that portrait. Perhaps it was me in my other life.

In 1981, Bruce and I visited the Maya archeological site of Tikal in Guatemala. We climbed the two major excavated pyramids. The third and tallest was eroded and covered in dirt and vines. Climbing was permitted but, frankly, was very difficult without steps. The tour bus stopped for the climb.

A seventeen-year-old boy and I climbed the pyramid in the rain and muck. We had to hang onto vines and use any tree root available to help us get a foothold. I was unbelievably determined to reach the top. It was as if there was some force or desire pushing me.

Once at the top, there was a stone square temple and bench inside. I sat on the bench alone and viewed the jungle and two other pyramids. The view and feeling were amazing. I never wanted to leave that place. I just wanted to melt into the surrounding jungle. It felt so eerily comfortable and familiar.

I felt something brush my side. I turned and saw Bruce!

He had been behind me all the time.

I asked, very surprised, "What are you doing here?"

"If anything happened to you, I could never explain it to your parents."

I looked out to the jungle. "I love it here."

"I can feel that you do."

"I never want to leave."

Bruce took my hand after a long few moments. "We gotta go back."

Hand in hand we worked our way down the pyramid and back to the bus. Once we were on the bus and driving away, Bruce said to me, "You know, you looked different up there."

"Different?"

"Your eyes were glazed. It was the worst I've ever seen you. You were gone, you know. Really way out there. I knew I had to pull you back."

I knew he was right. There was something powerful and profound I experienced up there on that pyramid. It was as if I was looking into my own past. Who knows if I would have seen myself or discovered something about this life, some issue that needed solving. I do know that I felt that same kind of melding into another dimension that I had felt in the creek when I fused with the light.

Though I have had other experiences with departed family members and loved ones, this early experience of mine at the creek in the woods set a divine framework around my life. I know there are many more people who have met with angels or divine spirits in their early childhood and who, like myself, either were told not to speak the truth to their parents or knew better than to talk about angels and divine lights . . . to anyone.

For so very long, we have remained silent for fear of retaliation, mockery, or, worse, being ignored. Well, the divine side of our lives is not ignoring us. There is so much to this life that we don't understand, and if we, as individuals, do not speak up, so much information will be missed when we are gone.

AUTHOR'S NOTE: I am including a bibliography that Suzi included in her package to me. Some of these publications are quite esoteric and some are intensely scientific. I thought you should have the option of deciding if any or all of it is of interest to you.

Andrews, Mark. "String Theory: The Stuff of Dreams and Matter," *Orlando Sentinel. Yakima Herald-Republic* 83, no. 362. 1986.

Atwater, P.M.H. *Coming Back to Life.* Ballantine Books, New York. 1986.

Newton, Michael. *The Journey of Souls: Case Studies of Life Between Lives.* St. Paul: Llewellyn Publications, 1994.

The Urantia Book. Chicago: Urantia Foundation, 2008.

Wolf, Fred Alan. *Parallel Universes.* New York: Simon & Schuster, 1988.

SECTION TWO

Heaven, Paradise & the Crystal City

HEAVEN, PARADISE & THE CRYSTAL CITY

A S ANCIENT AS THE STORIES ABOUT HEAVEN ARE, THIS IS a new area for me to explore in my books. When I personally visited the Crystal City during my own near-death experience, I had not heard much about such a place at the time. I had my childhood visions of what heaven must be like, with lots of clouds, angels, and saints, but to actually be in such a place was more than enlightening; it was life-changing.

What has astounded me in the years since then is the huge number of people who have seen what I have seen and more.

Some people have been told by angels or other spiritual beings that they are in "heaven." Some have been told the name is "paradise," and some are shown a "crystal city." Though the names are not the same, what is fascinating is that these descriptions appear to be the same place.

I have met some experiencers who actually have seen "pearl-encrusted gates" before entering heaven. For years I thought this was simply an extension of a belief system of the particular person while alive on earth. I no longer discount such visions but rather accept them as part of the scene some of us will see.

I remember my mother's elderly Aunt Sadie just before she died not only mistaking me, when I was four years old, for my mother (when Mother was a child) but also stating only moments before her death that she was seeing heaven. She said that "everything is so green."

How many times in movies and literature have we all seen and read about dying people who say that heaven is green? Or that they see a green valley? Innumerable.

With so many near-death experiences now that doctors and paramedics with modern technology can pull us back from the brink of death, we truly are seeing accurate glimpses of the after-life. These stories are the facts about heaven as evidenced either by the people who have died and gone there and returned to life to relate the story to us, or by those who have been taken to heaven by a deceased family member or friend or by an angel.

This section, then, is, as always, my effort at fitting together these puzzle pieces to give as much information as possible from which you will be able to draw your own conclusions. I will continue to chronicle these events as I come into contact with others who are generous, kind, and caring enough to share them with me and, ultimately, with you.

NEW HOME IN HEAVEN

I'M GOING TO TAKE SOME TIME OFF FROM WORK SO THAT I can be with you, Mom," Richard Ramirez said to his mother as she lay in the hospital.

"You don't need to do that," she said weakly.

"I do, Mom. I want to spend this time with you," he said with tears in his eyes, "because there isn't a lot of time left for us."

"Okay." She was quite weak and tired as she nodded.

"I want you to always remember, Mom, that we will always be together. Nothing, nothing will ever separate us. I promise you that." Richard leaned over and kissed her cheek.

"I'll remember."

"You promise?" he asked.

"I promise."

"Okay, then you rest tonight, Mom. I'll be here tomorrow, and we'll spend the whole day together."

"All right," she said. "Tomorrow."

"I love you, Mom."

"I love you too," she replied with a smile.

Richard walked out of the hospital that Wednesday night, 1998, not knowing it was the last time he would see his mother alive.

When Richard got home, he went to his bedroom and got ready for bed. Sleep came after a short battle.

In the middle of the night, a bright light filled the bedroom. Though his eyes were closed, the light was so strong he could nearly see the light through his closed eyelids. He opened his eyes.

"Mom?"

Richard was engulfed with a loving presence he knew instantly was his mother.

As he looked just past the bed to the other side of the room, he saw his mother standing within the bright sphere of light. She simply stood staring at Richard.

The light filled the entirety of the room. It covered Richard, and then it was as if the light was inside Richard. He had become a part of the loving light. He was filled with love.

He dared not take his eyes off his mother. She continued to stare at Richard and now had a concerned look on her face. Her countenance was exactly the same as it had been those last moments he'd seen her in the hospital.

The light continued to fill the room. While Richard was still looking at his mother, he suddenly disappeared.

Where she had been standing, there was now nothing.

"Mom! Don't go!"

Silence answered him.

Quickly, Richard looked at the digital clock. It was 4:11 a.m.

In the morning, the hospital called Richard to tell him that his mother had died sometime shortly after four in the morning.

Richard knew then that his mother had come to him to say good-bye.

Throughout the preparations for the funeral, the service, and the burial, Richard's concern for his mother mounted. He did not like the fact that her face had revealed a great deal of consternation when she had visited him in his bedroom.

A few days after his mother died, Richard was in bed, tossing and turning, unable to sleep due to his worry about his mother.

Finally, just as he slipped into slumber, his mother again appeared in the bedroom. This time she reached out to him.

"Come, Richard. I want to show you something," she said happily to him.

In the flash of an eye, Richard was transported to his mother's new home.

This "new home" was truly paradise. Richard saw rolling hills covered in soft, luscious green grass that swayed in the wind. The area was profuse with tall, beautiful trees and meadows of wildflowers.

Richard's mother took his hand as they walked over the hills. Remarkably, his mother did not appear to tire at all during their trek, though Richard remembered her laboring to walk up and down the hills. However, the wind blowing in his face was calming and soothing. The further he walked, the more wild-flowers came into view.

In the distance, Richard could hear a stream or river flowing.

Finally, they came to a river. There, Richard saw several ladies were sitting on the rocks.

Richard's mother walked into the water and stretched out in the water. The river was not rushing nor pushing her along. It flowed gently over her.

The women on the rocks began asking Richard's mother questions about people they all appeared to know in common.

How was so and so? Had she talked to so and so?

Richard's mother always answered that the person in question was "fine."

He took note of the fact that these women conversed with her with a great deal of familiarity. He surmised that they might be his mother's family members or friends who had died before her. It would then make sense that they would all be together and be concerned about each other's welfare.

Richard was overjoyed that his mother was so happy in her new life. His days of worry and concern could be put behind him. During this time, Richard felt his mother's love for him fill his soul. She loved him a great deal to come to him in this way to make him aware of her new life.

Finally, his mother got up out of the water, came up to him, and took his hand.

"We have to go back," she said.

They walked back over the hills away from the river and her friends.

When Richard woke up, he remembered the experience with unusual clarity. He, like others who have visited the other side of this earth-reality, knows that he was not merely dreaming. He knows that his mother had, indeed, come to him and that his experience was real.

AUTHOR'S NOTE: I asked Richard if he could smell any flowers when he was on the other side, and he stated that he did not. The wind in his face was quite real, however. He also stated that the water in the river was crystal clear. When his mother laid down in the water, it did not disturb her position in the least, though prior to their being at the river, when he was walking over the hills, he could *hear* the river flowing or the sound of the river's water from a great distance.

Dream of a Heavenly House

AUTHOR'S NOTE: This story was submitted by Jack Jones. It is only a snippet of a view of heaven, but again, it is important.

LOUISE JONES OF GLENDALE, CALIFORNIA, PASSED FROM this earth in May of 2005. Years ago, however, she experienced a profound and haunting dream.

In the dream, Louise found herself on the other side, or in heaven. She described often to her family that she saw a house with an inordinate number of rooms. The building itself was unusually bright and reminded her of "diamonds," because the light was many faceted. She stated that the colors were vibrant and that she saw hues and tones she had never seen before in her life.

In particular, Louise described a huge room filled with books of all kinds. She referred to this room as the "library." Interestingly, this room was several stories high, with rows upon rows of books.

She also describes the floor of this building or house as being nearly hot in temperature when she walked on it.

Louise also saw fantastic gardens with flowers of indescribable colors and shapes. Many were nothing like what exist on earth.

Wherever she turned, she was struck with how beautiful everything was.

When Louise awakened, she described the experience to her husband.

"This was no ordinary dream. It was far too real to have been just a dream. I've never experienced anything like it."

Jack states that years and years after this dream took place, his mother still talked of the experience as if she had truly been to heaven. She told her children never to fear anything and to never be afraid because she had seen a glimpse of heaven. She knew in her heart that there was an afterlife, and she knew that they would all someday be together again in that beautiful place.

Jack also tells the story of his sister, Linda's, tenth birthday party at the family home. There was so much excitement with all the guests, the decorations, the cake and ice cream, that Linda naturally became a bit overexcited herself.

Linda started jumping on the living room couches, going from one to the other, knowing fully that she was misbehaving and would most probably get into a lot of trouble with her mother. However, it was her party, and she just didn't want the fun to stop!

Hearing the shouting and laughing and the other children telling Linda to stop jumping, Louise came running into the living room.

"Linda! Stop that—" Louise entered the room and stopped dead in her tracks. She stared at Linda, who appeared to freeze nearly in midair.

Linda stopped jumping and stared back at her mother.

Louise's jaw dropped open, and her eyes widened to saucers, but she didn't say a word. Rather than scolding her daughter, she spun on her heels and walked out of the room.

Because the look on her mother's face was one Linda had never seen before or since, decades later, Linda asked her mother why she never reprimanded her on the day of her tenth birthday.

Louise smiled at Linda and said, "When I ran into that room to discipline you, I saw a bright golden halo over your head. I'd never seen anything like it. It just hovered over your head. I was speechless."

"So am I, right now," Linda replied.

"It was a reminder to me that God does love us at all times in our lives, no matter what we do. We are all God's children."

Linda laughed. "Even when I was jumping on the couches."

"Always."

TRANSPORTATION TO THE CRYSTAL CITY

AUTHOR'S NOTE: On March 13, 2006, I was a guest of George Noory on the *Coast to Coast* radio program. George warned me that after the three hours on the air talking about *Divine Nudges*, my newest book on angels, my email would get a lot of hits. Sure enough, the next day I had hundreds and hundreds of emails, enough to crash my site. Fortunately, I was able to retrieve every single email and download them. What is fascinating to me even now was a simple email from Michael Woodard that asked, "Did you see a mountain range during your near-death experience?"

It had been fifteen years since my near-death experience, and until Michael asked me this specific question, I had completely forgotten about the mountain range. I sat down and wrote out some notes, recalling everything I could about the mountain range: its distance from the city, the color, and its approximate location.

Two months later I set up a telephone conference with Michael, and we talked about this mountain range. When we compared notes, it was astounding how many facets of our experiences were the same.

I N MICHAEL'S EXPERIENCE THERE WERE TWO PARTS TO HIS dream sequence. The Crystal City is the second part of that dream.

On earth, when Michael would normally wake up in the morning, he was slow to awake, being groggy. In the dream, however, he woke up instantly. He was lying on his left side, which he normally did in bed as well. He propped himself up on his left elbow, and as he opened his eyes, he could see a clear blue sky with a few white clouds. He was instantly filled with the feeling of peace and contentment. There were no aches or pains as was normal on earth when he would awaken. He was struck by the fact that the temperature was absolutely perfect. It was not too hot or too cold.

He noticed right away that he was lying on a flat surface of some kind, which was covered with soft, brown leather padding. This platform was floating in the air and was about two miles high over the city. As he looked downward, he could see green grass and vegetation on the earth, but he also noticed that there were clouds beneath him as well.

At no time did he feel any fear whatsoever. He had no fear of falling and no vertigo. He felt very secure, and he knew that nothing was going to happen to him.

"Wow, this is high up!" Michael stated to himself as he looked forward in front of him and a bit off to the left to the city.

From this vantage point, he judged that the platform was approximately three to four miles away from the city.

He was impressed with the fact that the city appeared impec-cably clean. He saw reflections off the buildings, as there was a great deal of sunlight. At first he was trying to determine if the materials that built the city were very shiny metals such as stain-less steel or if the walls were made of glass.

The city looked very futuristic. There were tall, slender buildings and some shorter, dome-top buildings. He saw sweep-ing rooftops as well as sharp spires. He also saw flying buttresses such as were used in medieval and Gothic cathedrals on earth.

He was struck with the thought at the time that a great deal of it looked like the science fiction book covers he remembered from his childhood. Overall, he thought that the architecture was not like anything that we are familiar with here on earth.

The city extended from his left to as far left as he could see, as if it reached into the far horizon. On the far right ran a range of mountains, which seemed to stretch forever. The city ran up to the foothills of the mountain range.

The mountains were far away and appeared brown in color because of the fact that they were quite a distance from his vantage point over the city. He could see no details such as trees on the mountains or any kind of other vegetation. He saw neither water-falls nor any rivers on the side of the mountains.

Michael was still on the platform at this point, which was moving straight toward the city. He could see a very tall tower. At this point, he was about two to three miles from the city and still one to two miles high. The tall tower was not particularly wide in diameter. He judged it to be about thirty or forty feet across, thus quite narrow. The platform pulled up to the tower just as if it were docking on a space station.

Around the perimeter of the building was a catwalk. As Michael stepped out onto the catwalk, it was at this point that he realized there were other souls on the platform with him. He sensed that there were thirty to forty souls, although he could see only a handful of them.

At the moment that he stepped out onto the catwalk, a woman who appeared to be in her early to midthirties met him. She did not give a name. She was dressed in a white robe that resembled ancient Roman or Greek togas. He was struck by a pattern that ran up and down both seams of the toga. These were interlocking black letters that appeared edged in gold accents. This design also went around the hem of the toga, which was sleeveless. Michael also remembers that this woman's hair was long, straight, and dark, but he does not remember any of her other features.

She greeted Michael very kindly, and at this point, he and the others were transported to a room within the tall tower.

It was at this point that Michael awakened.

In my conversation with Michael, he said to me that all of his life he had been not just a skeptic but also a cynic about spiritual matters, other realms of existence, and the afterlife. However, about five years ago, he began experiencing obviously more than his fair share of just such information. He states that today he has become very spiritual indeed.

I thank Michael for sharing this extraordinary experience with me.

FLIGHT TO HEAVEN

AUTHOR NOTE: Mary's story is important because she clearly states that her experience was what she believed was a dream. As we have discussed many times previously in both *Angel Watch* and *Divine Nudges*, angelic messengers often visit human beings in dreams. Dreams appear to be a gateway between our world and the heavenly realm of existence or the world of the afterlife. As always, I will keep as much as possible to Mary's original story, told in her words.

MY EXPERIENCE HAPPENED IN A DREAM. THIS WAS NOT an average dream. It was very, very real. I remember nearly every detail quite vividly. I especially remember that at the end of the dream I felt myself go "whoosh" back into my body. This was a very unusual feeling. Also, as I awoke, my entire body was vibrating!

I refer to this dream as my "flying dream." I was thirty years old at the time. In my dream I was suddenly aware that I was floating. The next thing I knew, I was flying! I was holding the hand of someone whom I understood to be named "Zig Zag." I do not know who he was for sure, but I think that he was an angel. I still can remember his face. He had the nicest smile with big dimples. I was able to fly as long as I held onto his hand. Well, we went soaring up and up above the clouds and into the universe—into space. I know that it sounds crazy, but I was able to look down and see the earth very clearly.

We continued flying through space and came upon what I guess you would call a planet. As we got closer, I could see a huge city gleaming, and there appeared to be lights everywhere! I remember commenting, "I am so surprised that there are lights!"

Zig Zag replied, "Well, we need to see, of course!" He said this rather matter-of-factly.

I remember that the city seemed to glow or glisten. It was wonderful. I felt very honored that I was allowed to be there. I do not remember going down into the city or meeting anyone else. I believed I was simply brought there to observe this city and know in my heart and soul that it did exist.

The next thing I knew, I felt the "swoosh" and was back in my body, which was vibrating all over. When I awoke, I felt like it had not been a dream. It was far too real. I will never forget that incredible feeling of flying. I was as light as air and was soaring through the air! I certainly have had a desire to fly ever since.

Where did I go? I am not sure. Is Zig Zag my guardian angel? I do not know. I will tell you that I felt very safe with him. Was this a near-death experience? Well, I was perfectly healthy and woke up on my own. I am not sure what the vibrating was all about. I have since done research about out-of-body experiences and near-death experiences. I have read about people feeling a strong vibration all over their bodies as they awoke.

I was so excited about this experience that I wanted to share it with my mother the next day. I was surprised at her response, because she seemed to get very upset. She told me that she did not want me to "go flying" anymore! I'll never understand her concern, since I thought the dream was wonderful. Magical! Over the next several weeks, she would bring up the dream, saying that it really worried her and she did not want me flying again. When I asked her why, she would just say, "Please don't do that anymore!"

I had the dream in the early spring of 1994. My mother was healthy and fine. She became suddenly violently ill on Memorial Day weekend and died on the 4th of July of that year. I have always wondered if I had the dream so that I would be able to share my experience with her. I hope that my experience was given to me in order to guide her on her journey.

Many years later, I had an even more incredible dream. Again, it was very real. Thus, I don't believe it was actually a dream. I believe I was there.

In the dream, I was taken into a great hall, and everything

in the world was explained to me. I was given all knowledge and understanding. When I woke up, I remembered that I had been given the answer to everything, but I could not remember any of it. Again, my research has shown me that this happens to many people who have near-death experiences. At one minute you are filled with all kinds of knowledge, but once back on earth, it's gone.

However, I was left with a sense that everything was all right and as it should be. Everything in the world made sense. I had such a feeling of peace and contentment. I have kept a part of that feeling with me ever since. It is like part of me has an understanding—way down deep inside. I know I will be fine.

MYTONS

AUTHOR'S NOTE: This story and a second story, "Radio Dad," included in this book, come to me from Nancy Rapchak, who now lives in New York City. At the time of the incident described here in "Mytons," thirty-three years ago, she lived in Hessville, Indiana. Nancy's father was Mike Rapchak, a fairly famous big band disc jockey in Chicago for about fifty years. I actually remember listening to Mike when he worked on WCFL Radio and WGN Radio. Ah, those divine nudges never cease to keep bringing all of us together who are meant to help each other.

IT WAS IN THE EARLY SEVENTIES WHEN NANCY RAPCHAK was a mere thirteen years old and a freshman in high school. Over the course of that year, Nancy attended several parties at the home of John Graff, who was seventeen years old, a junior, and the lead singer of a band called Train City Blues Band. Nancy had a typical adolescent crush on John, but whenever she saw him or had the chance to talk to him, she was speechless. Other than uttering a few standard greetings, she didn't have the social expertise to take their encounters much further.

John was always cheerful and pleasant toward Nancy. He would smile and make a stab at small talk, but inevitably someone would come up to them and break up the conversation, and John would excuse himself, leaving Nancy alone, wistfully watching him converse with other kids.

That particular summer, John died. He overdosed on heroin.

John's drug use was a shock to Nancy. She had no idea he was a drug user and certainly knew nothing of his heroin use.

Though her romantic fantasies about John were strictly a figment of her imagination, he had always been nice to her. Though she was not all that close to John, in her way, she mourned his loss.

A few months after the funeral, Nancy was at home in bed. Neither awake nor quite asleep, suddenly she saw John. Standing to the right of her, he put his arm around her shoulder. Nancy states that even to this day, she can still feel the body heat she felt from him. Everything about the encounter was very real.

Straight ahead of them, she saw a bridge. A little lower than the ceiling of her bedroom, she saw a wonderfully beautiful place. She saw lush green trees and crystal blue sky. The colors were iridescent and gorgeous in their facets and tones. A wide, sparkling rainbow arched across the green, grassy hills. She saw and heard birds chirping.

John turned to Nancy and said, "Don't worry about me. I'm going to the Mytons."

John turned and pointed to the beautiful hills and meadows in front of them.

"John, I . . ." Nancy started to say, but John was gone.

The entirety of the vision had vanished.

She was alone in her bed.

"What in the world are the Mytons?" Nancy asked herself.

Several days later, Nancy met her friend Phyllis, who lived in Highland, Indiana, and who also knew John. Nancy explained her visitation to her.

"I know this sounds so silly, but I think I was visited by John's ghost a few nights ago."

Phyllis chuckled. "It's not silly at all. Don't you remember me telling you that after my brother died both my mother and I saw some pretty strange things in our house?"

"Do I ever! You told me that you saw flowers jump out of the vases on your mantle. And the pictures flew off the walls every now and then. I remember one time, I slept on your couch, and I was terrified that those flowers were going to come flying at me!"

"I absolutely believe in the afterlife. And I believe that our loved ones come back to visit us."

"I keep trying to tell myself it was all a dream," Nancy said. "Maybe I was really asleep."

"No. It was real," Phyllis replied staunchly.

"How can you be so sure?"

"Because," Phyllis answered, "he used the word 'Mytons.'"

"Yeah. What's that all about?" Nancy asked. "I've never heard of the Mytons."

"'Mytons' was the word John used to describe the afterlife."

Chills ran down Nancy's spine. "I saw it! I really saw heaven! It was fantastic—clean and pure and so beautiful it nearly hurt my eyes. It was . . ."

"Paradise?" Phyllis smiled.

"Yeah. It was paradise and I really saw it. I guess I should thank John. What a gift." Nancy smiled.

"A very loving gift," Phyllis agreed with a matching smile.

Nancy states that since the time of this incident, she has heard stories and read about numerous near-death experiences in which people describe the other side, or heaven, as being exactly the same beautiful, serene place she had seen during John's visitation. Though John's visit happened over thirty years ago, Nancy states that she remembers it "like it was yesterday."

SECTION THREE

Visitations from Departed Family

VISITATIONS FROM DEPARTED FAMILY

THE VISITATIONS IN THIS SECTION ARE PROBABLY THE most common, and most of us can nearly expect to have one or more of these experiences in our lifetime. In my past books on angels, I have retold many stories about a family member coming to visit the living. The family member is usually, but not always, a younger, healthier version of themselves. Almost always, the messages received are to tell the living that the departed one is happy in heaven, or on the other side; that they are looking over the living and that they continue to love the living.

Sometimes the departed return either to ask forgiveness for a wrong they have committed while on earth or to forgive the living relative for a wrong that the living committed against them. Again, almost always, the point of the latter is to allow the living relative to rid himself or herself of guilt over the wrong done.

Forgiveness is an ever-present theme among angels and the departed. If you feel that you should let go of a grudge toward anyone or a group of people that you have held for a long time, do it now. There are no guarantees that if you walk out of the door of your home today, you will return alive. Life is uncertain. It truly does turn on a dime. That is a lesson so many of us are learning in these precarious times of terrorist activities, increasing danger in our cities, and even the escalating numbers of debilitating, life-threatening diseases. We may be living in a modern age with lightning-speed technology, safety features on our cars, and unfathomable medical breakthroughs, but the unpredictability of life that ancient and medieval man endured has never really gone away.

So many times we receive angelic messages to give us hope. The departed loved ones want us to be happy. They tell us to live our lives in joy. They want the best for us.

Although television shows and films may utilize the horrific and sensational dark side of death to increase their ratings or box office numbers, the real truth is that the other side is truly a "love-oriented" place and experience.

The reports I receive from others who have been visited by departed family members are filled with kind and loving words. Even warnings that are given are dispensed with a need from the departed soul to help, even to save their loved one.

So great is the love that is being generated toward all of us from all our deceased relatives that it behooves us to say a little "thank you" to them from time to time for watching out for us. They go a lot out of their way to try to contact us. It's not that much for us to acknowledge them with a kind thought as well.

A MESSAGE FROM RICHARD

AUTHOR'S NOTE: This story was submitted by Ralph Hollenbeck on May 1, 2006.

IN 1997, RALPH WAS DATING A LOVELY WOMAN NAMED Barbara Coen, whose husband had suffered a very sudden heart attack just prior to Christmas. The doctors had not been able to do much for Barbara's husband and had put him on life support. Shortly thereafter, he was declared brain dead, and Barbara was forced to make the horrendous decision to leave him on life support or have him taken off.

Barbara chose to have him taken off the support system, since there was no chance her husband would revive at all, even with the support.

Barbara had been widowed a little over six months when she met Ralph. He knew from the onset of their relationship that Barbara was still feeling very emotional about her decision to take her husband off life support. He understood and tried to give her comfort and friendship. When Barbara asked Ralph one day to accompany her to her husband's grave in Loveland, Colorado, Ralph graciously agreed.

They took some flowers, and after Barbara placed them on the grave, she and Ralph stood silent for a few moments, both of them caught in their own thoughts and prayers.

After a few minutes Barbara said, "You died so suddenly. I wish you were able to talk to me."

Ralph took her hand and smiled at her. She gave him a wan but thankful smile in return.

They drove back to Barbara's home in Estes Park that day. That same evening, Barbara received a very odd phone call from a stranger.

"Are you the former Mrs. Richard Coen?" the man asked.

"Yes, I am," Barbara answered. "Why do you ask?"

"I know this is going to sound really weird, but as I was driving down Highway 81 between Columbus, Nebraska, and Norfolk, Nebraska, I saw a very shiny object in a ditch by the side of the road. It's not my habit to stop for something in a ditch. It could have been a soda can for all I knew. But this was extraordinarily shiny. It had a brilliance like I've never seen. I realized it was gold that was shining. I felt absolutely compelled to stop my vehicle and see what it was."

"What was it?" Barbara asked.

"A Bible!"

"I never heard of a gold Bible," Barbara said.

"It was the gold gilt on the edges of the pages that had caught the sun's reflections and shone so brightly."

"I see."

"Well, I looked in the Bible, and it had the name Richard Coen as the owner."

"That's very bizarre. I was married to Richard for seven years, and I know very well he did not own a Bible."

"Well, I called the Norfolk newspaper and reported that I found the Bible."

"The Norfolk Newspaper?" Barbara asked. "That's where my daughter worked, but that was years ago."

"Well, the people there sure remember her and had her number. And they called her to get your number. That's how I found you."

"That's a lot of work because both Lisa and I have moved."

"It's okay. And I'd like to send you this Bible."

Barbara thanked the caller, and within a week she received the Bible. Richard's name was indeed on the inside. The Bible must have been in the ditch for months, but the truly remarkable thing was that there was no weather damage—snow, rain, or sun—to the Bible.

Ralph said to Barbara, "I believe your prayers have been answered. You did the right thing, and Richard is in heaven. Your answer couldn't have been plainer than that Bible finding its way to you."

ANGEL ON MY SHOULDER

AUTHOR'S NOTE: This story was submitted by Janice Kozak of Charleston, Illinois.

JANICE'S HUSBAND PASSED AWAY FROM CANCER IN MARCH 1989. Understandably, Janice was racked with grief and felt alone and very sad. Her sole companion at the time was her chocolate Labrador retriever. During those initial weeks and months after her husband died, Janice walked endlessly with her dog, many times over thirty miles a week. During her walks she tried to deal with her emotions, yet she could not shake the loneliness that haunted her.

Janice's loneliness led to a prayer. "If I could just have a sign that I'm not alone, then I would know. Then I would have comfort."

One particular day, Janice was walking her Lab down a familiar street that had no sidewalk. Suddenly, she was aware of the noise of a loud car engine as it accelerated on the cross street ahead of her. She was approximately fifty yards away from the intersection at this time.

She continued walking toward the intersection and realized that the accelerating sound was growing louder still. At this point she heard the sound of a second vehicle, but it was traveling at the speed limit. The closer she got to the intersection, the more aware she was of two approaching cars, one that continued to accelerate and one still going at a normal rate of speed.

Janice was struck by the thought that the roadway on which she was walking and the speeding car was driving was no place for this car to continue to accelerate.

At twenty yards from the intersection, Janice suddenly felt strongly compelled to stop. At the moment that she halted, she felt a strong pull on her shoulders as if two hands were holding her in place. She couldn't move. She tried to make herself move, but her body stood stock still.

In those moments, she felt confused and a bit embarrassed to be standing alongside the road and not going anywhere.

For nearly a half minute, Janice remained rooted to the spot. The pressure on her shoulders did not ease up in the least. Her dog stood just as still as she did, as if sensing something unusual was happening.

Just as suddenly as the pressure on her shoulders had descended upon her, it disappeared.

Janice realized it was now all right for her to continue walking. During this entire period she was still aware of the sounds of the two approaching cars traveling on the cross street, which was now about twenty yards from her position.

Just as she began walking again, the first car came into view. This was the car traveling at normal speed. As it entered the intersection, it was followed and passed by the second car, which was still accelerating. The second car careened around the first car on the right, driving up on the shoulder of the road.

"How dangerous!" Janice said aloud. Then she watched the second car as it flashed past her. "Someone could get hurt!"

Because she had now arrived at the intersection, she crossed the street. Once she was on the other side, she looked back and was stunned by the fact that the careening car had driven up on the shoulder where she had been walking.

"That's not possible. If . . . if I had not stopped when I did, I would have been in precisely that spot where the reckless driver just passed that other car!"

Janice bent down and hugged her dog. "We were both saved. Someone is watching out for us."

Her dog licked her cheek.

"We are not alone at all." Janice smiled and hugged her dog again.

Janice had prayed often for an end to her loneliness. She doesn't know if the invisible hands on her shoulders were those of her husband or an angel or both. She does know that she has proof that no matter where she goes, she has someone who loves her to keep her safe and be her divine companion.

PENNIES FROM HEAVEN

KEVIN BLOCK'S DEARLY LOVED MOTHER PASSED AWAY from a very long illness in the year 2000. As would be expected, Kevin deeply grieved over her death because he loved her very much. She had been such a wonderful force in his life, and the absence of her laughter and comforting presence left a huge void.

At times, Kevin wasn't quite sure how to handle his grief, the pain was so great. After several weeks of mourning, Kevin prayed that Jesus would send him a sign that his mother was with God.

Just a short time after this prayer, Kevin and his wife bought some flowers and went to the cemetery to visit his mother's grave. When they got to the gravesite, they realized that someone had put pennies all over his mother's headstone.

"What is going on?" Kevin asked, a bit upset. "Who would do such a thing to my mother's marker?"

At first Kevin and his wife looked around to find the perpetrator, which in retrospect was ridiculous. Surely, a vandal would have been long gone.

Kevin looked at his wife and realized she was smiling.

Then Kevin began to smile as he looked back at the pennies.

"I can't believe it! 'Pennies from Heaven' was Mother's favorite song!"

"I know, Kevin. Isn't it wonderful?" his wife replied.

"What a fantastic sign! I prayed for this!" Kevin exclaimed.

"And your prayer was obviously answered," his wife said. "This is exactly the sign that your mother would have sent to us."

Kevin and his wife hugged each other and smiled as they said prayers for his mother.

As they walked away hand in hand from the cemetery, Kevin and his wife knew that they had been given a very rare gift, indeed. They had real proof that his mother was in heaven and that she was doing just fine. They believe that she is waiting for them, when they will all be reunited in the afterlife.

As the weeks and months have passed since this incident at the cemetery, Kevin and his wife have noticed that seemingly no matter where they go, they keep finding pennies everywhere!

Kevin and his wife are fine examples of keeping angel watch.

The angels truly are all about us at all times. Frankly, they are just waiting for a chance to get in touch with you, but you have to pay attention.

THE FIBER-OPTIC ANGEL

ALL OF US EXPERIENCE DEATH AND LOSS AT ONE TIME OR another in our lives. It's part of life. But in 2005, Gail Mitchell lost her father, her younger sister, an uncle, and an aunt within a four-month period. To say that she was having an emotionally rough year would be an understatement.

Gail told herself that all her dear ones were in a better place. However, what she knew logically did not lessen the impact of the enormous burden of grief that she felt every day.

Two weeks before Christmas, Gail attended an arts and crafts sale at the school where she worked. There she found a darling ceramic angel with very pretty wings.

When Gail got home that afternoon after school, she showed the little angel to her thirteen-year-old daughter, who replied, "It's really cool, Mom."

Though her daughter dismissed the little treasure, Gail liked it immensely. As she was about to place the little angel on the top of the entertainment center, she turned it over and saw a switch on the bottom. She realized that the pretty wings were actually fiber-optic lights. She turned the angel on to see it light up. Smiling to herself, she then carefully turned it off and placed it on top of the entertainment center.

Later that night Gail received a phone call from her other younger sister saying that her cousin, Randy, had committed suicide the day before.

Gail was inconsolable in her grief. Randy's death was nearly the straw that broke the camel's back. Gail felt she couldn't take anymore. Grief hung on her like a heavy mantle. It weighed her down like an oppressive tyrant.

Frankly, Gail was in shock that Randy would commit suicide. She just didn't understand why he would do such a thing.

"Why, Randy, why?" Was all she could ask.

Unable to sleep because she was so filled with grief, Gail

resorted to cleaning the house just to keep her mind off Randy. The last room she cleaned and straightened was the living room. Finally, exhausted, she checked the living room one last time, turned off the light, and went to bed.

However, sleep was totally elusive. For hours she stared at the ceiling, cried, and kept asking Randy why he would leave. Realizing that there was no way she was going to get Randy out of her mind, she gave up trying to sleep and went into the living room once again.

She sat down in the complete darkness thinking that if she did not turn on the light perhaps she would finally get sleepy and be able to go back to bed. Still, her thoughts were with Randy.

Looking up at the entertainment center at that moment, she saw a very faint light. At first she couldn't figure out what it was. Then she realized that the little ceramic angel had been turned on. The fiber-optic lights in the wings changed colors from red to blue to yellow to green. Just as she was thinking to herself how pretty it was and how glad she was that she had bought the angel, she realized that earlier she had turned the angel off! She also knew for a fact that her daughter had not left her bedroom since much earlier that evening. Because Gail had been awake all night, she knew that her daughter had not turned on the angel. In addition, her daughter did not even seem to like the angel.

In that moment, a deeply felt sense of peace filled Gail. Suddenly, she knew everything would be all right. She believed in her heart that either an angel or Randy was trying to give her a message that he was okay.

Gail got up, went over to the entertainment center, and looked at the bottom of the ceramic angel. Sure enough, the switch was on.

Gail went to bed that night thanking all of her deceased family members and her angels for coming to her and filling her with hope and peace.

As she lowered her eyelids and allowed sleep to overtake her, Gail was certain that she had seen the last of her angelic messengers.

However, the next morning when Gail walked into the living room, there, in the center of the room, was a bright, shiny penny.

Because she had so carefully cleaned the living room the night before, she was absolutely positive there had not been a penny smack dab in the middle of the carpet.

At that moment, her daughter woke up and came into the room to join her.

"Sweetheart, did you see that penny in the middle of the room before you went to bed last night?"

"No, Mom. I didn't."

"And you didn't put it there?"

"Why would I do something like that?"

"It's just very strange that a penny would be right there in the middle of the room. I thought perhaps you had dropped it."

"Sorry, Mom. It wasn't me."

To this day, Gail is convinced that she received not one but two messages from heaven. They came at precisely the time when she needed them most. She is ever thankful.

My Two Moms in Heaven

NOT EVERYONE IS AS LUCKY AS CINDIE GILBERT, WHO was gifted in her life with both a loving adoptive mother and her biological mother. Though Cindie knew her biological mother for only a short period of time, when she died in 1983, only seven months apart from the death of her adoptive mother, Cindie was understandably deeply grief-stricken.

Both women suffered a great deal physically before they died. Cindie's biological mother died of cancer, and her adoptive mother had severe heart problems.

Obviously, the void in Cindie's life yawned before her like the vast unknown. With both of her mothers gone, she had lost both her friends and her counsel.

A few weeks after the last funeral, Cindie experienced an usually fitful night of sleep. At around four o'clock in the morning, Cindie had a most unusual dream. In the dream, if we can call it that, she saw both of her mothers. They looked incredibly real, and everything around Cindie was very vivid. It was like no other dream she had ever had in her lifetime. Both her mothers were smiling and looked very happy to see her.

Cindie's adoptive mother, in her life on earth, had only one arm. Interestingly, in the dream, Cindie immediately noticed that her mother now had both arms. In her earth life, she had a peculiar way of holding her right elbow, because she had lost her right arm just below the elbow. Cindie noted that even though she appeared with her arm intact, she still held her elbow in the same way as she had in real life.

It was her adoptive mother who spoke first.

"Cindie, I wanted you to know that heaven is very real."

"Is that where you are?" Cindie asked.

"Yes."

"We have come to bring you a message," her biological mother said.

"What is it?" Cindie asked.

Her adoptive mother replied, "Your life is about to change, and your lesson is to learn to accept that change."

"In what way is it supposed to change?" Cindie asked.

"In all ways it will change."

Cindie was really surprised at this information. As far as she was concerned nothing about her life needed changing. Then both her mothers said the oddest thing, which has stuck with Cindie all these years.

Simultaneously they both said, "Plant your garden."

"What is that supposed to mean?"

Again, in unison they both said, "You will know."

This exchange had taken quite a few minutes, and at this point, Cindie had become very curious about what else was going on around her mothers. She investigated the surrounding area because the entire room was glistening with a very bright light. Though the light was bright, it did not hurt Cindie's eyes. She noticed that there seemed to be a floor beneath them, but it was not the floor in her bedroom. In addition, she did not see her mothers' feet nor her own feet, and she felt as if all three of them were floating.

"Where is Jesus?" Cindie asked.

"Right here," they both replied.

"Am I allowed to meet him?"

"No, but if you look closely, you may be able to see part of him."

Cindie strained her eyes, and a vision of Jesus's feet came to her. She was surprised at how strong they appeared. He did not wear sandals. His feet were simply bare, and she did see scars on them. She was struck by the fact and the notion that his feet appeared very pretty, as they glistened with a light of their own. She was filled with elation that she had been allowed to have this small vision of Jesus.

By this time, Cindie had been speaking with her mothers for eight to ten minutes. She felt a profound sense of being loved unconditionally and that this place or dimension that she was experiencing had brought her pure bliss. She remembered thinking at the time that she must be dead and that she certainly did not want to go back to earth. Everything around her was gorgeous and wonderfully peaceful. It was truly paradise.

Cindie's biological mother must have picked up her thought telepathically because suddenly she said, "You are not dead and you cannot stay here."

"We love you very much, Cindie," both her mothers said in unison.

"I love you both. You know I do. I miss you so much."

In her heart and soul, Cindie knew she still had an obligation to care for her children on earth. She could almost feel them pulling on her.

"Cindie, it is time for you to go back now."

In a flash Cindie found herself in a tunnel, and while it was not brilliantly lit, it was not dark either.

She felt as if she were slammed into her body, and she immediately got up out of bed. Incredibly, she felt exhilarated and refreshed like no other day she had ever experienced in her life. Even though it was after four o'clock in the morning, she could not go back to bed.

Cindie states that after that night, everything about her life changed like clockwork, as had been foretold. She lost her job, her husband, and one of her sons. At the time, while she was going through these massive, life-altering changes, when she told the story of her vision to her coworkers and friends, they all commented that this had to be what "plant your garden" meant.

Cindie has a bit different take on what that phrase was to mean to her. She believes that she was supposed to make the best out of whatever life was handed to her. Today, Cindie's children are grown, and she no longer has a husband. However, she's not worried about what tomorrow will bring. She knows that both her mothers are on the other side and that they are very proud of her.

I believe that Cindie has planted her garden well.

RADIO DAD

AUTHOR'S NOTE: This is the second story from Nancy Rapchak. Nancy's father was Mike Rapchak, a famous big band disc jockey in Chicago for about fifty years. Mike passed away on March 27, 2006.

THREE DAYS BEFORE MIKE'S DEATH, NANCY SUDDENLY started appreciating the light in the dial of her thirty-year-old Technics radio receiver. The radio had been her possession for over twenty years, therefore her newfound interest in the light in the dial was an odd observation for her to be concerned with. For some inexplicable reason, she was drawn to the light and would stare at it for long moments. She was filled with nostalgia for the past, and memories of her childhood and later life filled her mind. However, she continued to be puzzled as to why the radio seemed to beckon to her.

The night before Mike died, while Nancy was talking on the telephone with a friend, she reached over and flipped on the radio. As she was staring at the radio, in about three seconds, the light suddenly went off. For days now, she'd been staring at this always-functioning illuminated dial and now, suddenly, it just went out. Chills crawled up her arms.

"That was my dad," Nancy said in hushed, reverent tones to her friend, as she felt a strong shutter rumble across her shoulders. She knew instantly something was wrong.

The next day, she received the news that her father had died.

Nancy flew from New York City to Indiana for the funeral. Because Mike had been a fixture in the Chicagoland area for over fifty years playing big band music on both WCFL and WLS radio, Nancy was overwhelmed by and grateful for all his friends and loving fans that paid him tribute.

Several days later, Nancy flew home to New York City. Looking out the airplane window and seeing Chicago fade in the distance, she thought of things that she had wanted to say at the wake, but at the time there had been nothing in her head except for shock and grief.

She noticed that in the armrests there were satellite radios where the ashtrays used to be. Fortunately, she had the entire row to herself. The radio to her right had no readout in the little illuminated window, but she still plugged the earphones in to see if they worked. She was surprised to hear the radio playing a country song. She changed the station to another country song. Because she had never used satellite radio before, she wasn't quite sure what she was doing. She kept pushing the left arrow.

Eight times she got eight different country songs on eight different stations, but there was still no readout in the little window to tell her anything about the stations, their call letters, or the song titles.

She then decided to try the radio to her left, which did have a well-functioning window display and which showed the stations' call letters. She paged through several stations and finally came to a sixties station. She heard the Tremeloes singing "Here Comes My Baby." Only a few seconds later, the station began breaking up for no apparent reason. To Nancy's way of thinking, she thought the reason that people had satellite radio was to avoid interference.

She then decided to put the earphones back into the radio on her right and see if she could find something besides all those country music stations.

The very second she plugged the radio jack into the outlet, the readout on this heretofore inoperable readout window flashed, "Glenn Miller, Glenn Miller, Glenn Miller."

"What in the world?"

Because her father had idolized Glenn Miller nearly all of his life, Nancy knew from her father's stories that the famous bandleader had died in a plane crash.

Dread filled Nancy's mind. She was suddenly terrified that perhaps her father was trying to tell her that her plane was about to crash. Terrified, all Nancy could do was stare at the readout.

Memories of her father telling her about Glenn Miller's life flooded her brain.

Suddenly the pilot came on the loudspeaker. She just knew he was about to give them instructions for the upcoming crash.

Nancy tore off the headset in order to hear the pilot. However, the pilot simply explained their cruising altitude and their estimated time of arrival into New York City.

When she put the headset back on, she heard a woman singing, "Something to Remember Me By." This was another one of her father's favorite songs. The irony of the title was not lost on Nancy.

Interestingly after the radio to her right had flashed "Glenn Miller" over and over, the readout suddenly ceased to work.

Nancy continued to listen to the big band songs and found that their words and music were strangely soothing. As she flew over Whiting, Indiana, where her father had lived, she started crying. She then heard Jo Stafford begin to sing, "There's No You." As they came in for a landing in New York City, the station played Lionel Hampton's version of "Flying Home."

In the past, while Nancy was talking with her dad, she would often say that she had never been able to figure out where home really was. Was it in Indiana where he was, or was it in New York City where she lived? He would always say, "This is home."

Nancy knows now that her strange experiences on the airplane, listening to a string of her father's favorite songs and seeing the odd on-again, off-again display window on the satellite radio, was truly no accident. Mike was communicating with her in the best way he knew how.

Above all, Nancy knows that her father was telling her that he was finally, truly home.

IRENE'S WATCH

AUTHOR'S NOTE: This story comes to me from Irene Wheeler. It is remarkable to me because, as you will see when you read this story, Irene has kept an angel watch all her life. Fortunately, for her and us, Irene kept her eyes, ears, and heart open to these wondrous moments when they occurred in her life. Irene's story underscores the fact that the life we live here on earth is only a small part of our soul's existence. She is one of those people who are able to look back on her life and put together these divine puzzle pieces.

IRENE WAS IN HIGH SCHOOL WHEN SHE EXPERIENCED HER first visit from someone who had crossed over to the other side. One of Irene's best girlfriends was involved in a car accident and died. Irene found it almost impossible to accept her friend's death. To Irene, they were all too young to die. Death had come too soon in Irene's young life.

Not long after the funeral, Irene's friend came to her one night in a dream. In the dream, Irene was astounded at how beautiful and peaceful her friend appeared.

"Irene, I wanted you to know that it was time for me to go back home."

"Then I'm happy for you."

"That's all I came to say."

When Irene awoke from the dream, everything that happened to her and that was said was incredibly clear. Irene states that to this day it is difficult for her to believe that it was a dream, because it was so real. There is no question in Irene's mind that the vision she saw was her friend's true spirit. This visitation was a validation to Irene that life does exist after this one we live here on this earth. What she didn't know was this was only the first of many encounters she would have with spirits and souls making contact with her from the other side.

Many years later, Irene was visiting one of her family members. She recalls that when she was with them, she experienced an inexplicable feeling of loneliness about them. It was as if somehow they were already cut off from this life. She believed that both her uncle and her brother-in-law were quite healthy. However, she had no idea how she was to relate this information to them or even if she should. She chose not to say anything, hoping that her intuitions were wrong.

Several months later, Irene's uncle suffered a massive and sudden heart attack and died instantly.

A few months later, her brother-in-law was diagnosed with terminal cancer. He'd had no prior symptoms and had always been healthy. However, the cancer overtook him quickly. He lived only a short eight weeks after the diagnosis.

Irene's longtime hobby was listening to a police scanner. A year after her brother-in-law's death, the scanner reported troopers talking about "leaving the body at the crossroads." Because her twenty-six-year-old nephew was over three hundred miles away that night, Irene did not immediately think that anything was wrong with him.

However, within minutes, her sister called and told her that her beloved nephew had been in an accident. Instantly, Irene knew in her heart that the victim the police had been talking about over the scanner that night was her nephew. He had died in a bizarre snow machine accident.

Years later, Irene's mother became gravely ill and was taken to the emergency room one night. During the time that the doctors were taking care of her mother, Irene stayed with her all night long. The doctors told Irene that there was no way her mother was going to make it. However, though Irene was concerned for her mother, she did not have the feeling that she was about to die.

"You're going to be fine, Mom. These doctors are the best. They're going to give you very, very good care. I just know that everything is going to be okay."

"Irene, I have to tell you that I see your father in the room with us. You see him, don't you?"

Irene looked around the room but saw no one. Irene squeezed her mother's hand. "I'm sure he's here. I think I told you that many times when I'm walking, I talk to him and tell him how much I miss him. Just last week I was walking, and I saw a man approach me with the most loving smile I can ever remember. It impressed me at the time that his smile was much like Dad's. There was an incredibly wonderful feeling that came over me when he said hello. I just know that Dad was trying to give me a sign that he was still around."

Though the doctors had believed that Irene's mother would not make it through the night, she actually lived for another eighteen months. Irene visited her mother in the nursing home as often as possible over those remaining months. Irene states that her mother had many near-death experiences and would often relate these experiences to Irene.

There were many incidents when Irene was in the room with her mother that her mother explained that they were being visited by deceased family members. All these visitations were loving and hope filled.

On one particular night, Irene's mother was very close to death. However, Irene heard her calling out and saying that she "wanted her body back." She was very upset and adamant about her situation. Obviously, she was not ready to go. It was another year before she would pass to the other side.

On the night that Irene's mother died, she told her daughter that she was being visited by nearly every one of her family members. Because Irene's mother was the last of her own family to be on earth, the room must have been quite crowded.

While Irene was speaking with her mother, she saw a "shadow" in the corner of the room. It lasted for only a brief moment, but it was one of those occurrences that can never be mistaken for imagination. Irene knew at that moment that most probably the "shadow" was her father.

"I'm glad that they are all here for you, Mom."

"Irene, there is something very important that they are telling me."

"What is that?"

"They want me to tell you that he is going to look after you and everything will be okay."

"God, you mean."

"Yes, God."

Tears spilled from Irene's eyes as she held her mother's hand. "Thank them for me, won't you?"

"I already have."

On that particular night, Irene knew in her heart that this time her mother was finally going to die. However, there was so much love in that room from all of the family members who had come to help usher her mother to the other side that Irene, herself, was at peace.

Though Irene misses her mother, she knows that her mother no longer suffers and is now with her family and loved ones in heaven.

SECTION FOUR

Vanishing Angels

VANISHING ANGELS

VANISHING ANGELS ARE ONE OF THE MOST FASCINAT-
ing phenomena I have encountered. When it first happened
to me, I did just as I expect most people do: I went into denial.
"That didn't just happen." I convinced myself that the entire
experience never took place.

The problem is that if you have ever been visited by an angel
in a dream or real life, you never, ever forget it. The experience
haunts you. Somehow, it becomes a part of your consciousness,
and no matter what you do, you can't make it go away. It comes
back again and again.

Vanishing angels do not come in dreams. They appear as
human beings and vanish from sight in seconds. These angels usually appear to save the human being from imminent danger. The
story from Donna Voll is particularly interesting because she was
not in any mortal danger at the time, but she was floundering in
her career. She needed guidance and had been praying to receive
a sign about what she should do. Donna got more than a sign. She
was visited by an angel who changed the course of her life forever.

Angel visitations are universal. By that I mean that angels are
not specific to any one particular religion. Nearly all religions on
earth describe some sort of angel "messenger from God" who
comes to earth to warn us, give us information, or relay a message
that is for a group of people.

Angels are also seen by people who have no religion at all or

71

have not been raised with a particular religious background. Like very young children who report seeing angels and talking with them, I find these reports utterly incredible. Again, it is so very easy for us to rationalize that what others have seen is simply an extension of their belief system. That they were "making it up" because they were in a crisis situation and their psychological need to have a respite from the emotional or mental pain produced an illusion or a hallucination.

That kind of thinking works for a while . . . until you have an angel show up literally in your office! Suddenly, your life is touched and your thinking is altered. Fortunately, not all of us have to have a near-death experience to wake us up. Sometimes, a vanishing angel will do.

TRUCKER ANGEL WITH A CB

AUTHOR'S NOTE: This amazing story of life and death on the highway during a winter storm is from Elizabeth Muelhaupt. Though it took place in 1978, the divine warning vibes of this story reverberate still today.

It is interesting to note that Elizabeth states she has been seeing angels since the age of three. Thanks to Elizabeth's ability to keep her heart open to angelic intervention, we have her story to help guide us during frightening times.

In this book we will include another, more recent story from Elizabeth.

December 2, 1978

I WAS LIVING IN DES MOINES, IOWA, WITH MY HUSBAND and two children, Jim, five years old, and Jeff, two years old. My husband was a car dealer, and we had to drive two cars to California.

The night before this trip, I experienced overwhelming feelings of apprehension that were so disturbing, I actually mentioned them to my mother. Knowing me as she did, she advised me to postpone the trip. My husband, however, would not listen to me. He had to get those cars to California.

He drove a Lincoln Continental, and I drove a 1978 Cadillac. Both were heavy cars for the time, which should have been some reassurance for me, but it wasn't. I started praying the minute I got behind the wheel.

We were only a few miles into the trip when the weather turned horrific. It was a traveler's nightmare. Sleet and freezing rain turned the highways into a skating rink. Before I reached highway marker number 8, my car went out of control. In seconds,

I was off Interstate 80 and was in midair pumping my brakes. The car landed over 100 feet off the highway.

I was shaking, and my legs felt numb. I couldn't believe I was still alive.

"Thank you, God. Thank you!" I said aloud.

My husband saw the accident in his rearview mirror. He pulled over and backed up his car to the location where my car had landed. He told me to get out of the car so that we could check for damage.

I walked around the front of the car and saw not a scratch or dent anywhere, except for a small dent the size of your baby fingernail under the chrome rocker panel.

I then pulled myself up to the Interstate by hanging onto overgrown weeds. It was then that I realized how far down the embankment I'd gone.

Finally the highway patrol arrived. Then came the tow truck.

The patrolman stopped traffic, and it took over an hour to get the car pulled out of the ditch and onto the Interstate.

Finally, the Iowa highway patrolman asked me, "Who are you?"

"Excuse me?" I didn't know what he was asking since he had all our pertinent information.

"Lady, you should not be talking to me at this moment. How in this world did you keep the car from rolling over or flipping?"

I was still so shaky, I simply stared at him. The full impact of what could have happened to me was just beginning to register. I was no Mario Andretti. I was more than lucky. I had been saved. He knew it. I knew it.

When the car was towed to a truck stop eight miles away at Council Bluffs, Iowa, my husband insisted that I get back into the car and we continue westbound.

"This is too dangerous. Let's just go back to Des Moines."

"No way. I have to get these cars to California. Period."

We got back in the cars, continued down I-80, and drove through downtown Omaha. At this time, the weather turned fierce once again. The sleet was coming down in sheets so thick I couldn't see out of the windshield. I put the driver's window down and hung my head outside to see if I was staying in the painted lines on the highway. The cars in front of me and behind me were playing dodge 'em. We tried to stay away from each other so as not to collide.

When I finally reached the west end of Omaha, the freezing rain lifted. Then the snow started falling. I saw car after car leave the Interstate and head for safety. But not us. My husband was not about to stop.

By three in the afternoon, we were near Kearny, Nebraska. I had not eaten breakfast or lunch, and I felt we all needed to get something to eat. I moved over to the right lane with my right turn signal on. My husband followed me.

When we stopped, I begged my husband to stop this insanity. I remembered that we had a friend who lived in Kearny, and we could wait out the storm. "I could call him."

"We've lost so much time because of your accident and the weather, we will not stop here."

Nightfall came about four thirty. By this time I couldn't tell if my husband was in front of me or behind me. We were in the middle of a whiteout.

For those who don't know, except for an ice storm, which we'd already encountered, there is nothing more frightening than a whiteout. The snow comes down in what looks like white sheets. It's impossible to judge distance, and even seeing the front of one's own car hood is impossible. At nightfall, it's deadly for a motorist. I could not see exits or even the road at all.

Suddenly, I wondered why my car wasn't moving . . . at all! I had apparently driven my car into a snowdrift or something.

Out of nowhere a trucker came by. Because I was on my CB in my car and had been using it, I heard, "Lady in the Caddy, you are in the median. If you don't put your foot on the gas right now slowly, you will be buried for the night."

I immediately put my foot on the gas pedal, and like magic, the car lifted up and was somehow, inexplicably, back on the Interstate!

"How is that possible?" I asked myself.

I had no idea how the car came up like that. It was as if the angels had lifted the car and me back onto the highway.

The truck driver was a godsend. I knew that. He pulled in front of me.

All of his lights around the top of the truck were so bright, I had no trouble finding him. Finally, a beacon to light my way.

"Where are you heading?" he asked on the CB.

"To Cheyenne, Wyoming," I answered now that I was driving again.

We drove a few miles and then the CB came on again.

"It's impossible for you to see the exit because of the fog. I will turn on my right signal to show it to you. You're doing just fine."

"I can't thank you enough," I said. "I'll follow your signal."

In a few minutes, just as promised, his right signal went on. As I turned off the Interstate and began the exit, I quickly looked back to wave to my rescuer and saw that the huge, brightly illuminated truck was gone.

I mean gone. Vanished. Nowhere in sight.

"Okay," I said aloud to myself. "Maybe he disappeared into the fog. I'll just try the CB."

I picked up the CB and called his "handle." There was no answer. I tried it again.

Silence.

"Hey! I want to thank you!" I shouted into the CB.

Eerie silence.

Goose bumps raced down my spine. I knew what had just happened.

"That was no trucker. That was an angel."

I believed it, knew it with every cell in my body.

I continued down the ramp and one block to the left was a Best Western Hotel. I parked out in front near the office.

I walked inside, and the woman at the reservation desk said, "Oh, Elizabeth. We've been waiting for you."

"What?"

"Your husband and another dealer from Iowa are in room 111 right around the corner."

The next morning we left to continue the trip. It was a better day, and somehow we made up for lost time. We stopped in Lake

Tahoe and then went up into the Sierras. It was dark, and I could not see the side of the road. My headlights were so covered with grime and gunk that I couldn't see a foot in front of the car. I was looking for a place to pull over and clean off my windshield and headlamps.

For the third time on this one trip, I was touched by an angel . . . literally.

I felt something tap me on the right shoulder. It was a distinct pressure. There was no mistaking it.

At that moment, I had the idea to put my turn signal on, as it would light up the road enough for me to see if it was safe to pull over.

As I got out of the car to clean my windshield and headlights with snow from the side of the road, I saw three cars pull over as well.

"Liz, is that you?" One of them called.

I recognized the voice as one of the other dealers who was traveling with us from Iowa to deliver the cars.

"It's me."

"We can't see ahead of us, and we wondered why you were pulling over."

"I can't see either. But let me get this straight. You were using me as your guide?"

"Who else?"

At that moment I realized I had been counting on the angels to guide me. Maybe these fellas knew that as well. All I know is that the entire trip was a nightmare, but it was also proof to me that I am divinely protected. No matter what. I used the angels to guide me, and the others thought I was their angel. Maybe I was. Maybe that's the answer. God uses all of us, angels and man, to help each other.

ANGEL RESCUE IN LOS ANGELES

AUTHOR'S NOTE: This story was sent to me by Dottie Clark. I think it's interesting that Dottie's residence is Port Angeles, Washington. Truly, she's surrounded by angels all the time.

I T WAS 1957, AND I WAS VISITING MY PARENTS IN THE LOS Angeles area. I borrowed my father's car for some reason, which I can't remember now. I had my three-month-old daughter in a portable bassinet that hooked over the front seat of the car, which left her sleeping in the backseat.

I was in the fast lane of the freeway when I heard a horrible noise coming from under the car. I was scared to death and worked my way over to the nearest off-ramp, which happened to be in the absolute worst part of town.

I pulled into an old, beat-up garage. There were a lot of "gang type" boys hanging around (even though I don't think they had gangs back then). It just seemed to be a hangout.

I stopped the car and was bent over the steering wheel shaking and crying. I didn't want to get out of the car and was wondering what in the world I was going to do.

All of a sudden there was a pecking on my window, and I looked up to see a very nice looking Caucasian man dressed in a suit. He showed me a badge, and I rolled the window down just a little to talk to him.

"The tread has come off your tire. I want you to lock the door and stay in the car. I'll take care of everything."

I can't remember if they fixed the tire or put on a new one. My mind is foggy about that. I didn't have any money with me and was going to ask him for his name and address so I could send him the amount of the bill.

When the work was finished, he came up to the window and

told me to "leave right now."

My daughter started to fuss and cry. I turned around to see if she was okay, and when I looked back, he was gone. I looked around everywhere and could not see him anywhere. He had just vanished!

I was so terrified, I simply did as he said and left.

Now, whether it was an earthly or heavenly angel, I do not know, but I have always suspected that it was my heavenly angel.

LOST DOG

AUTHOR'S NOTE: This story was sent to me by Barbara Constantine of Nantucket, Massachussetts.

SEVERAL YEARS AGO, I WAS TAKING CARE OF MY FRIEND'S very old, deaf, and blind dog. One particular night he had wandered off my property. I had no idea how many hours had passed since the dog left. I contacted the police, and they told me they would have my neighborhood patrol car keep an eye out for the dog.

I was frantic. After checking around in the nearby vicinity for the dog, I finally got into my car and searched for the dog in the early morning fog. I could barely see a thing. It wasn't much use to call for the dog since he was deaf.

I used my cell phone to contact the police again, but they still had not found any sign of the dog.

I didn't know what to do. I was frustrated and afraid for the dog. I said aloud, "I need help! This dog has been gone entirely too long!"

I decided to turn my car around and pulled into a driveway, which was lined with a thick row of hedges and bushes.

Suddenly, a man popped out of the bushes and startled me.

"May I help you?" he asked.

"I'm looking for my lost dog. I can't find him anywhere, and he's deaf and blind."

"Does the dog have Cambridge tags?" he asked.

I was surprised by his question. "Yes. Yes, he does!" I answered, my heart leaping with hope.

"I think you'll find him a couple miles away. Down that road."

"You saw him?" I asked.

"Yes. He was moving too slow for me to bring him back here.

I just came back to call for help."

"Thank you! Thank you very, very much!" I replied excitedly and then backed out of the driveway and headed down the street in the direction the man had indicated.

This time, because I knew I was in close proximity to where the dog could still be, I started calling his name.

Clustered at a bus stop on the corner, a group of about five people heard me calling, and they all pointed further down the road.

I drove a bit further down the road, looking in all the yards, both front and back. It was as if I were hunting with an instinct I didn't even have.

I finally found the dog in a backyard.

I hugged his neck, and he licked my face. I was so happy to see that dog.

As I drove back the way I'd come, the people waiting for the bus were gone. As I passed by that corner, I wondered to myself, how was it that all of those people knew where the dog was? He was in a backyard and not all that visible to anyone walking down the street. Common logic told me that it was possible for one of those people to have seen the dog, if they were looking into everyone's backyard as they walked toward the bus stop. However, it was not logical that all of those people would have seen the dog.

I had to look very closely at every front and backyard to find him. Plus, I knew what I was looking for. Interestingly as well, I didn't see any other dogs in the area at all.

Then there was the matter of the man in the bushes. Where did he come from? He appeared so oddly, and later, when I checked with the police, he had not called them. Why hadn't he called them before I'd arrived? Was he waiting to give the information to me?

Years later I mentioned the story to an employee at the local animal hospital. As it turned out, he knew the owners of that house where I'd pulled into the driveway very, very well. All this time, I assumed the man was the owner of that house, but the animal hospital employee told me he did not fit the description of the owner. In addition, he knew of no one fitting that description who was related to the owners or even one of their friends.

The more I thought about the strange man in the bushes, the more I was convinced he was an angel.

It's good to know angels watch over us and our loving pets.

Earth Angel Rescue

AUTHOR'S NOTE: The following story was submitted to me by Patricia J. Smith of Arizona. I have kept the story essentially as Patricia wrote it for her voice and emotions to come through. Though I have experienced nearly the same kind of angel as did Patricia, as I present this story to you, the reader, I am filled with awe at these instantaneous apparitions from angels at precisely the moment when we need them. All we have to do is ask.

IT WAS THE BEGINNING OF THE HOLIDAY SEASON. YOU know the time—when holiday parties abound and what to wear is your focus. However, this holiday season was going to be my first since my husband walked out and left the children and me on welfare. Parties, cheerful holiday greetings, and dressy attire were not in my consciousness.

I had landed a position as receptionist at a software company in Maryland right over the Virginia border. It didn't pay all that much, but it got me out into the world again, where I needed to be for my own sanity. I was invited to a Christmas party by one of the women in the human resource department. At first I declined with whatever excuse came to mind. But I was met with resistance and convinced it would be good for me to get out and socialize. Despite my fears, real or unreal, I accepted her invitation.

This all took place in the 1980s, when most moms drove those gas-eating station wagons, and I was certainly one of them. The afternoon of the party, I stopped and put in a few dollars of gas. I figured it would be enough to get me to the party and back. The event was north of Washington, DC, in a Maryland suburb. I was coming from a town south of DC. I anticipated it to be a thirty- to forty-minute trip each way. I planned not to stay late. Driving after dark alone was something I didn't want to do.

The party was lovely, actually. People were pleasant and cheerful. Still, I felt out of place and really would have preferred to stay home with my two teenage sons. I made a point of leaving around 10:00 p.m., not too late—before the bad guys take over the streets!

I snaked around the area a bit before finding the "beltway" but somehow missed the entrance to the beltway south. Instead, I was heading north, which I didn't notice for almost twenty minutes.

"Great," I said to myself. "I'm heading toward Baltimore and my gas gauge is almost on empty." It was a fairly rural area. The exits weren't well lit, so it was difficult to distinguish if there were gas stations open. Ultimately, I just got off an exit and followed the road over the beltway.

It was pitch black, with no streetlights of any kind. Part of me was starting to worry that I might run out of gas in the middle of nowhere.

In the distance, I could see a poorly lit, run-down convenience store standing by itself on the side of a narrow road. It looked like something out of the *Twilight Zone* TV shows of the fifties and sixties.

I decided to pull in and ask the cashier for directions to the nearest gas station and a south entrance onto the beltway. As I entered this little store, I instantly knew I was in big trouble. Here I was, a woman, all dressed up and in need of assistance. It was obvious I was lost and alone and out of my element.

Behind the counter a young man was speaking with two other young men, who appeared to be purchasing some snacks. They all stopped talking when I walked in. They looked me up and down as if I had just landed from another planet. They weren't smiling.

At that moment I said, "Could someone help me find my way back to the interstate?"

Instinctively I knew I was in danger, extreme danger. Whether instinct or just a reflex, I said to myself, "God, I need your help."

The second that thought flashed through my head, an elderly man with gray hair and a kindly face walked out from behind the shelves.

The three young men seemed surprised to see him, as if they didn't know he was in the store. I know I certainly hadn't seen him.

The elderly man was dressed in a simple beige jacket and gray slacks. Overall, his appearance was very neat, and he had a distinguished air about him.

He walked by me without making eye contact and said, "Follow me. I'll show you the way back."

He just kept walking toward the door and into the parking lot. I immediately followed him.

The three young men still had not uttered a word. They just stared with their mouths hanging open.

I proceeded to get into my car. I turned the car on. I noticed that the gas gauge was now registering "empty." All I could think of was that I would never make it back home. My other thought was, "How do I know this guy is to be trusted? What if he leads me straight into harm's way?"

In the next second, I felt a rush of superpowered faith and decided to trust in this old man. There was something about the gentle look on his face that eased my mind. But the most incredible thing was that when I was around him, he had a distinct calming presence about him. He didn't frighten me at all.

I followed this kind man in his beat-up, old car for forty minutes south to my exit in Northern Virginia. I glanced at my exit sign and then went to signal him a "thank you," but he had disappeared. He and his car were gone, where only a split second earlier he had been in my sights in my rearview mirror. He had absolutely vanished into thin air!

Despite driving on empty for almost forty minutes and many miles, I made it safely back to my house. I got out of the car, kissed the driveway, and thanked God. It took a number of weeks before I could mentally process the whole experience. I kept asking myself, "Who was that elderly man who came out of nowhere and brought me home safely?" Did God really care what happened to me? So many questions, but in time the answers came to me.

Many years later, when I think of this "earth angel," tears

come to my eyes. Do angels really exist? The answer is YES, absolutely YES! We are all special in the eyes of God, who provides angels to watch over us.

I have shared this story with many people. There are believers and there are cynics. I guess not until you meet your own angel do you realize they truly are there by your side at all times.

I consider myself blessed to have had that experience, and I hold it close to my heart. It still gives me comfort to know I'm really not alone, ever! Nor are you!

TICKET SCALPING

IN SEPTEMBER OF 1979, MICHELE LYNN WENT TO MADISON Square Garden in the hope of scalping a ticket to see the rock band The Who. The concert had been sold out for weeks, but she believed there was a small chance that she just might find that elusive ticket.

A scruffy man approached her and told her that he indeed had a couple of tickets. Because she was such a fan of The Who, she allowed her excitement over the possibility of buying the tickets at a not-to-be-believed low price to cloud her otherwise rational judgment. Her guard came tumbling down, and she believed him absolutely that he had the tickets.

"Okay, I'll buy them," Michele said.

"You need to follow me," the man replied. Then he began motioning for her to follow him as he started to walk away.

"Where are we going?" she asked.

"To get the tickets."

"Okay."

Michele began to follow him, not realizing that she was in danger. All she could think about was the fact that she was getting these tickets at a great deal.

The man continued walking and took her deep into Penn Station. He walked several paces in front of her. She had to walk rather briskly to keep up with him.

Finally, she followed him into what looked like a dark locker room.

Dread filled her body. She knew instantly that something was not right and that this man had lied to her and did not have tickets to sell her. Still, she did not know what to do.

She walked into the room but kept her back to the doorway.

Just as panic filled her completely, out of the blue, she glanced over her shoulder and saw another man in a dark, business-length coat walking by. The man reminded her of an angelic character straight out of a Hollywood movie. Her instincts were to trust him.

Actually, there was nothing unusual about this man that she should notice, because nearly all the men in Penn Station were dressed in business attire.

The man's eyes met Michele's eyes. He must've noticed her panic. He immediately stopped and said, "Do you need any help?"

Michele did not even answer. All she could do was keep her eyes locked on his.

Without another word, the man in the business suit walked into the room and took her arm. He led her out of that dark room and away from her assailant. They walked through the terminal to a very safe place. Now, Michele was surrounded by hustling commuters.

The second that Michele expelled a deep sigh of relief, she turned to thank the man who had just saved her life and realized that he had vanished into the crowd.

She stood on tiptoes, trying to find him. She looked everywhere and in every direction, but there was no sign of him.

Michele learned the hard way that she had been far too gullible when she trusted the man who was going to sell her the tickets. She realized with this experience how easy it is for young people, and especially children, to be wooed away from their homes and places of safety by kidnappers, sexual deviants, and murderers. Michele is a bright and intelligent young woman. However, because of her enthusiasm about seeing her favorite rock band, her emotions at the time were nearly her undoing. She is extremely aware of how important it is for all of us, young or old, to pay attention to our surroundings and to others who would do us harm.

Michele was lucky and blessed that the businessman had come along when he did. There are those that would tell her this was an amazing coincidence, but she does not believe in coincidences anymore. Perhaps she was saved at that time and has gone through that experience just so that she can tell this story for others to read and to learn from.

There is no question in my mind that what Michele experienced was an angelic intervention.

PATRICIA'S SURFER ANGEL

WHEN PATRICIA WAS SIXTEEN YEARS OLD, SHE AND HER family went on a vacation to St. Augustine, Florida. At this time, there were seven children in the family, so it took a great deal of planning on her parents' part to organize these trips. Everyone was quite excited about this adventure to the ocean. It was the first time that Patricia had ever seen the ocean, and when they finally arrived in Florida, the Atlantic Ocean in all its magnificence was everything Patricia had dreamed.

While Patricia's parents sat on the beach taking care of the two youngest children, the five older kids all jumped in the surf. Everyone was diving and romping, splashing and playing.

Because Patricia was extremely adventurous and a very good swimmer, she found that in no time she had put a great bit of distance between herself and the shore. When she looked on shore, she was shocked to see that her parents appeared as only tiny specks on the beach. So enamored of the experience of finally being in the ocean, she had completely forgotten all the ground rules and warnings that her parents had given her. She completely forgot about tides and undertows. She suddenly realized that the waves around her were quite high and growing larger by the moment.

She decided to head back. However, it seemed that no matter how hard she swam, she was not getting anywhere. It was then that it dawned on her that the tide was pulling her out as she was trying to swim in to shore. For quite some time, she kept battling to make her way, but all she accomplished was getting tired. Her muscles began to ache. Then they began to tighten and spasm.

Then she began to panic.

Her younger brother, Rick, came up beside her because he had followed her out, and now they were both in the same predicament. They struggled together, but they made no headway. At this time, Patricia realized that she was going under the water's surface more than she was spending time above it. Choking and sputtering, she did not want her brother Rick to know that she was afraid.

Continually, she tried to keep her spirits up and to give him encouragement that they would make it to shore and everything would be just fine. She realized that she had started to feel euphoric and was actually beginning to believe what she was telling her brother. At the time, she did not realize that this euphoric feeling is something that all people who are drowning experience.

She did not realize that she was at the point of drowning. Patricia suddenly felt someone grab her arm. At first she thought it was her brother, but as she came up from beneath the water's surface, she realized it was not her brother at all.

He was beautiful—golden-tanned, tall, and lean. His hair was sun-bleached blond, almost to white. He wore white swim trunks, and he clung to a white surfboard. Patricia couldn't help thinking that he looked like a movie star out of a beach movie.

"Hold onto the surfboard, and I'll help you get to land," the surfer said.

"I'm exhausted," Rick said.

"It's okay. I'll paddle you to shore," the gorgeous rescuer replied.

Patricia held on to the white surfboard and tried to help the man paddle them ashore, but she, too, was exhausted.

Finally, they got close enough into shore that Rick and Patricia were able to finally stand up in the hip-high water. After only a few feet, Patricia stumbled onto the shore. She turned around to think the gorgeous rescuer, but the man had vanished into thin air.

"Where is he?" Rick asked.

"He was just here!" Patricia exclaimed.

"That's just nuts! I was just holding on to the surfboard," Rick said.

"I know. I just heard him splashing. He was right behind us."

While Rick went to find his parents and tell them about the incident, including the story about the surfer rescuer, Patricia sat down on the shore and scanned the entire beach for a sign of the rescuer.

She waited on the shore for several hours, looking at every single man she saw, but there was no sign of him. She saw men of all sizes and types with every kind of surfboard imaginable. She saw men dressed in black trunks, blue, red, and lime green trunks. However, not one single man was dressed in white bathing trunks.

For the remaining week of the vacation, every single day, Patricia went down to the beach searching for the man who had rescued her and her brother from near death. She never found him, and she never had a chance to thank him.

Patricia believes that she and her brother were saved that day by an angel. There simply is no other explanation for such an incredible and miraculous event.

VANISHING CABBIE ANGEL

AUTHOR'S NOTE: As is often the case, angelic interventions can happen in the flash of what seems to us, upon retrospect, a nanosecond of our lives. Osie's story of his mother, Grace, and her angelic intervention is short, but the incident was very real, and it certainly impacted me.

I T WAS OVER TWENTY YEARS AGO WHEN OSIE'S MOTHER, Grace, went to visit her friend. Though Osie wasn't there at the time, he explains that his mother and her friend got into an argument. Grace had wanted to use the telephone but had declined to state whom she was calling. Her girlfriend, who obviously had an issue with jealousy, demanded to know if Grace was calling her friend's boyfriend. Grace insisted she was not interested in this woman's boyfriend. However, all of Grace's assurances fell on deaf ears. The result was that Grace's friend demanded that she leave immediately.

Not one to take abusive behavior from anyone, Grace gathered her things and walked out the door. Once outside, Grace's shock and anger dissipated, but she absolutely refused to go back inside under any circumstances.

It then dawned on her that she had no money for a bus or a cab. She just didn't know what to do.

Before she could even think much more about the situation, a taxi cab pulled out to the curb. Grace was astounded because to her, the cab appeared out of nowhere. The driver rolled down the window and asked her if she needed a ride.

Grace politely explained that she had no money with her.

"That's okay. I'll take you home anyway," the cab driver said.

Grace shook her head, "You don't understand. I'm not sure

that I even have any cash at my house, and it's well over three miles."

The cab driver smiled, "You look like a nice lady. I'd be glad to take you home."

"Well, God bless you."

Grace got in the cab. As they drove, they chatted about a few things, and all the while Grace felt comfortable and safe with this man.

When they got to Grace's house, she thanked the man profusely.

She got out of the cab and walked the short distance to her front stoop. She turned around to wave to the man and realized that he had vanished from her sight.

She looked up and down the street, but she saw no one. No cars and pedestrians. No one.

It was all the more odd to Grace because she knew that she should have heard his cab pull away from the curb if he had driven away.

A taxi and its driver just do not vanish into thin air, Grace reasoned to herself. Unless she had been saved that night by an angel.

SECTION FIVE

Animals as Signs of the Afterlife

ANIMALS AS SIGNS
OF THE AFTERLIFE

THESE STORIES WERE A SURPRISE TO ME. I HAVE BEEN A pet owner of both cats and dogs nearly all my adult life. When my cats, Cinnamon and Spice, died within a month of each other, I was mournful for months. However, I don't recall seeing them in dreams or having the feeling that they were trying to visit me.

When my golden retriever, Beau, died suddenly at the age of twelve, I can honestly say that I still have not recovered from his passing. I have seen Beau many times in dreams and have even had "waking" glimpses of him around me since the time of his death. I always feel that he has come to let me know that everything is okay and that he is waiting for me when I die.

I know that many people feel the same way about their pets as I do and that having a pet die can be as traumatic as losing a human relative. Our pets are family members. They are our children.

What surprised me were the stories you will read in this section, not only about pets and their visitations but also about deceased family members "sending" animals to the living as a sign of life everlasting. I received hundreds of these stories. I had no idea this phenomenon was so widespread. I've included the best and the most illuminating of these stories here for you.

I believe that it takes a sharp eye and keen sense of angelic connection for most of us to realize that when these "odd" situations take place, there is more going on than just seeing a bird or a particular cat. We have been blessed at such times with a divine message.

We are not alone.

We are unconditionally loved for who we are.

We will be reunited with our family when we pass over to the other side and live in love in heaven.

CLEOPATRA

AUTHOR'S NOTE: This story and information was submitted by Susan Menkes Simonson in August 2006.

I HAVE A FRIEND, JACKIE OAK, WITH WHOM I ATTENDED LA Porte High School. We have been fortunate to remain friends all these years. As I was putting together this information about Egypt, Jackie telephoned me and commented that ever since she met me in 1960, all I ever did was talk about Egypt. Even when I was on the school newspaper, whenever I had the chance to write about something, I chose Egypt. She even possesses a poem I wrote about Cleopatra, the name of my cat.

In May 1999, I spent three weeks touring Egypt. I took the Nile River cruise to tour the archaeological sites. I had the special opportunity in Luxor to visit the Valley of the Queens in addition to the Valley of the Kings. Only one hundred people daily are permitted inside the tomb of Queen Nephertari, Pharaoh Ramesses II's first wife.

Visits are limited to ten minutes.

I entered alone, and the previous group had left. No one else joined me. The paintings on the walls are so beautiful and touching, they absolutely took my breath away.

I started to quietly cry, I was so moved.

The guards looked at me, but when they realized the impact the tomb was having upon me, they motioned for me to stay.

Because of their kindness, I remained in the tomb for over thirty minutes. It was the most marvelous tomb, and during those minutes, I felt a very close connection to Nephertari.

I distinctly heard a male voice say, "I will bring you back."

Of course, I can never be sure, at least not until I die, but I felt that it was possible I could have been Nephertari. While I was there, I felt that Bruce, my husband, might have been Ramesses II. It is quite possible that others in that eloquently spiritual place may have felt the same things I was feeling and thought the same things. There are those who also would say that perhaps both of these people were my ancestors and that could be the reason for the profound and nearly magnetic tie I felt to both of them at that time.

It's interesting to note that for years prior to my trip to Egypt, over the bed in our master bedroom hung a painting of Nephertari offering jugs of wine to Isis. The painting is depicted on Egyptian papyrus as well.

In the years since my travels to Egypt, I have continued to read everything I can about Egypt and Mexico in particular, because of my experiences in those countries. I am so incredibly and inexplicably drawn to both places, just as I continue with metaphysical and quantum physics explorations as well.

In 2001, we brought a new kitten into our life, and so, because of my love for anything Egyptian, I named our kitten Cleopatra.

She's a lively little girl, and an Egyptian breed. She's grey and white striped with huge eyes and perky ears. She has a fun little face that reminds me of an innocent child. She is the third cat I've owned.

My first cat was Anna, a large, black and white female who lived with us for nineteen years. When she died, I had her cremated, and her ashes rest in an antique brass urn on our fireplace mantel.

One day while Cleopatra was playing on the scratching post previously owned by Anna, I decided to take some snapshots of her. I took twenty-five shots.

When I took them to have them printed, I asked for one of those composite sheets as well that show the sequence of the shots for future reprinting purposes.

When I looked at my photos, I couldn't believe it. The first shot is one of Cleopatra playing on the floor.

The second shot is one of Anna playing on the scratching post.

That's right. You read that correctly. The second shot was a very clear photograph of my Anna, who had been dead for twelve years and whose ashes rest on our mantel.

I was so shocked, I wrote to Dr. David Wishart, an oncologist, who did not believe in an afterlife, but we shared an interest in Egyptology and mummification. However, he didn't have an explanation.

I wrote to John Hart, a professional New York photographer and specialist in lighting. He wrote back to me: "The cat photos are too much. So a dead, cremated cat reassembles her ashes into physical form on a photograph after twelve years?"

I couldn't have said it better myself.

When something like this happens, to me it appears to be spiritual truth. It is as if God is trying to show us that our lives go on and on and that there is another life, another world, beyond this one; yet we humans have such an ingrained mental mechanism that seems to always find a way to explain away anything and everything we can't yet measure and don't understand.

I believe that Anna, my cat, has a life beyond this one just like I will. I've read a great many stories about those who have died and returned to their life on earth and related stories about their pets greeting them on the other side. I think Anna was trying to tell me she is right here with me. She may be living in a parallel universe or dimension right next to me, but I can feel her love. And she can feel mine.

MICHAEL AND THE SPARROW

AUTHOR'S NOTE: This story, submitted by M.L. Mooney, was interesting to me because it covered a six-year span of time. Most of us are unaware of signs from the divine. I believe that it is important for us to be open and continually aware of unusual circumstances or incidents at the time of a dear one's death. By allowing ourselves to remain open to angelic intervention, it is amazing how much more we see and learn about what life is . . . from a spiritual perspective. Michael is that special kind of person who knows that God is working in his life at all times. Not only is his faith strong, but it also helps him recognize even the smallest miracle.

IN DECEMBER OF 1991 MICHAEL LOST HIS FATHER, LOREN. His mother, Hazel, was incredibly devastated by Loren's passing, and nothing Michael or anyone did seemed to console her. Though she went through her days performing her daily tasks, Michael could tell that her grief was deep and profound.

One day while they were at the cemetery saying a prayer over his father's grave, Michael turned to his mother and said, "Mom, I do not believe that the good Lord would want you to suffer in the way that you are. Your grief seems to have taken over every part of you and your life. I'm really worried about you. I also don't think that Dad would want you to be this depressed and despondent."

With tears in her eyes, she looked at him and said, "I just don't know how to come out of this."

Michael's heart nearly broke as he watched her shoulders shudder as she cried. He put his arms around her and held her. At that moment, Michael silently asked the Lord to give him the words that would ease his mother's emotional pain.

"Mom, I don't know how this is going to happen, but I know that God is going to give us a sign. I know that sign will be something you are meant to see and understand. It will be for you and you only. And when you see it, you will know that God is taking care of us and Dad."

They said another prayer together, and then Michael had to leave. His mother remained at the grave in order to pray a bit longer.

As Michael walked away, he had great trust in the Lord that he would take care of everything and that his mother would be fine.

One week later, when Michael went to see his mother, she was very excited to see him.

"Michael, it's happened. It has really happened!"

"What are you talking about?"

"God sent me a sign. It was just like you said he would do," she said.

"What kind of a sign?" Michael asked.

"Whenever I have gone to your father's grave since the day we both prayed for a sign, I have seen a large bird fly directly over my head. Even when the sky was totally devoid of any kind of bird or a cloud, I saw this bird. That bird was never there before this, Michael."

"I have to admit, Mom, that I don't remember seeing any large bird at the cemetery."

"Your father used to say that because he suffered so horribly from arthritis and gout that he felt as if he were in prison. He longed to have the freedom of a healthy body again. This bird is a symbol to me of freedom from your father's kind of disabilities. I believe he is happy and healthy in heaven."

"I see what you mean."

Six years later, Michael's mother was diagnosed with cancer. Because she required a great deal of care, during her last month on earth, she moved in with her sister in a nearby city. This house had a beautiful, screened-in porch built on to the home. During those last days, Michael's mother would sit on the porch and read her Bible. She died on October 22, 1996.

About a week after the burial, Michael's aunt came home from the store and found a little sparrow trapped in the screened-in porch. This incident is extremely profound and unusual because there was no way for that sparrow to get into that room in the first place. There were no tears or splits in the screen, and the door had been locked from the inside. There had been no visitors to the house, and there had been no deliveries. The little sparrow was a sign to Michael, his aunt, and his whole family that his mother was doing just fine in her new life in heaven.

As Michael moves forward with his life on earth, he is deeply aware that as simple as these signs would be to many people, for him they are solid reassurance that both his mother and his father are together and are watching over him always.

Joyful Earth Partnership

AUTHOR'S NOTE: Divine interventions are not always about us. Sometimes, we are called upon to help and give aid to our planet, animals, our pets, our forests, or other living matter that coexist with us. Sometimes, as well, it takes a message from our angels or God to cause us to wake up. I am printing Claire Papin's article she wrote for her Joyful Earth Partnership column, which originally appeared in *The Indigo Sun Magazine* in June 2006, with her gracious permission. I think you will find her unique dream that recently occurred important and eye-opening. Perhaps you will see as I do that we are all responsible for the future of this beautiful blue planet.

"One Step at a Time"

IT IS SOMETIMES CHALLENGING TO IMAGINE JUST HOW much one person can do that can possibly make an impact on issues of surmounting proportions, whatever the issues may be. It's tempting not to even try to put forth the energy. And then, there is the unstoppable sensation of "go for it" that rolls in like a strong tide where there's no turning back. I recently had one of those tides roll in, and there's been no turning back since.

In early May I had a dream that I was overlooking a shallow pool of water with a large number of dolphins who had died and been washed ashore. There were many people, some of them marine researchers, standing around trying to figure out what had caused their deaths. I noticed that the dolphins were of many breeds and found myself walking among them to see if there were any survivors that I might be able to help, offer nourishment, or take care of in some way.

I called out to the people I saw around me that we need to give the dolphins food and to please help. I looked at the people with urgent anticipation for support for the dolphins who might have survived. Many of them were so caught up in astonishment by the magnitude of this perplexing catastrophe that they could not even respond to my plea.

When I awoke from the dream, later that very day, I saw a television news report that stated off the east coast of Africa, there were approximately five hundred dolphins that had died and washed ashore. Researchers and scientists were trying to figure out what had caused their deaths. They said that they had run tests and ruled out poisoning. Currently, they would be checking to see if there had been any sonar testing in the area.

The next day, I saw another report in the newspaper saying that the death count had risen to nearly eight hundred dolphins. Interestingly enough, they also reported that the stomachs of the dolphins had been unusually empty. Sometimes this can happen with mega sounds from earthquakes or sonar from war ships, which can cause the dolphins to regurgitate their food.

Needless to say I was incredibly saddened by the event. I felt as if the dolphins, in such a large number, were trying to tell us something. I also knew, due to my long years of experience in the communications field, that the media would probably not do much more with the story after it became yesterday's news.

I felt an enormous sense of responsibility to check into this further, and do what I could to keep the public informed in the hopes that, through awareness, we might be able to stop the possibility of another tragic event like this happening again. Not to mention, that we should take a look at whatever the message might be that the dolphins are trying to share with us, and see what action to take from there.

I immediately went into action and sent emails and made phone calls to every conceivable environmental group I could find. Just to name a couple who are moving forward: Care2 has agreed to share about the incident on their website, and the NRDC (Natural Resources Defense Council) is checking into the possibility of military sonar testing in the area. Communications are still building, and the list of support is growing.

There were some organizations that had not yet heard about the news report and were stunned to learn that so many dolphins had lost their lives in this tragedy. After sharing my experience about the dream, and the news I've picked up along the way, they all were very agreeable that this story should not fall by the wayside. A few of them decided to gear up for doing some of their own detective work.

I have to admit that I did not know what kind of reaction I was going to get in sharing with all these people the fact that I had experienced a pre-cognitive dream before the newscast was announced. I just knew it needed to be shared, especially since just two days after the event, there was an ocean earthquake off the nearby island of Tonga, and a tsunami warning for that area, as well as for New Zealand.

The support needed to keep these environmental groups strong is of great importance. For those of you who are interested, I am listing a few groups:

Care2 connects people who care (that's you!) with the organizations, responsible businesses and individuals getting results in helping make the world a better place. It's a big plan that touches on health, the environment, women's rights, spirituality, children's welfare, human rights and much more. www.Care2.com

Greenpeace is the leading independent campaigning organization that uses peaceful direct action and creative communication to expose global environmental problems and to promote solutions that are essential to a green peaceful future. www.Green Peace.org/USA

The Natural Resources Defense Council is one of the nation's most effective environmental action organizations using law, science, and the support of 1.2 million members and online activists. Their purpose is to safeguard the Earth: its people, its plants and animals and the natural systems on which all life depends. www .NRDC.org

I believe it's crucial for us to consider the symbol of joy

that dolphins represent, and how they often offer the important reminder to nurture and take care of our joy during this time of great transformation, as well as engage more deeply in our relationship with Earth in a joyful way.

ANGEL DOG MISSY

AUTHOR'S NOTE: Many of my readers will remember my stories about my three golden retrievers. For all those readers who have pets and are animal lovers, this story will tug at your heartstrings. Again, I thank M.L. Mooney for his lovely contribution to this book.

COMING HOME AFTER A STAY IN THE HOSPITAL IS DIFFIcult for anyone. For Michael, he'd been in the hospital much longer than anticipated. He, like most of us, was overjoyed just to be back with his own things around him and to feel the comfort of his own bed again.

Because Michael was still recovering, a friend brought him an "older" puppy to keep him company. The puppy's name was Missy. She was a very friendly and pretty puppy, taking to Michael right off the bat. However, Michael was soon to discover this was more than the average dog.

On several occasions while Michael was asleep at night, his oxygen mask would come off his face.

As if she'd been trained in ER procedures, Missy instantly knew something was wrong when the oxygen mask slipped off. She went to the bed and woke Michael up so that he could replace the mask and receive the necessary oxygen.

But that wasn't all.

Even more mysteriously, Missy awakened Michael at those times when his blood sugar dropped dangerously low. Again, Missy was there to rescue her master.

Seeing or sensing that Michael's oxygen mask was askew or off his nose was one thing. Sensing that Michael was in danger due to an internal problem was quite another.

To Michael, it seemed more than appropriate to start calling Missy his guardian angel.

Strangely enough, about a week after Michael started calling Missy his guardian angel, he noticed a small blonde patch, the size of a half dollar coin on Missy's left flank.

At the time, Michael thought that Missy had simply laid down on a recently bleached kitchen floor. It made sense that strong bleach could be the cause of the discoloration.

However, not long after this, a second patch showed up on Missy's opposite flank.

Over the next month, both these patches grew to resemble angel's wings.

Michael's landlady and friends not only witnessed the transformation as it took place, but all of them also have commented often on how these patches actually look like angel wings.

Missy should be a reminder to all of us that God is always with us, loving us and protecting us.

DAD'S BLUE JAYS

AUTHOR'S NOTE: This story was submitted by Sherry McKelvey of Lubbock, Texas. Over a decade ago I was a "literary ambassador" for the Lubbock Chamber of Commerce and spoke at dozens of elementary and high schools in the Lubbock area. I still cherish those days when I was a judge in a city-wide fiction and poetry competition. When I saw this letter from Sherry and read her sweet miracle, I was strongly impacted. Though it is a simple incident to see a particular bird, there is nothing simplistic about being divinely contacted. Fortunately for us, Sherry had "the eyes to see."

TWO YEARS AGO, I MOVED BACK TO MY PARENTS' HOME to help my mother take care of my father, who was dying of lung cancer. I closed up my own home here in Lubbock and took my two dogs with me. I was with my parents for nearly two months. I have to admit, it was physically exhausting and emotionally draining on all of us, and I wouldn't have missed a minute of it for the world.

The night my father fell into a coma, my mother and I stayed up with him all night. We both sensed he was very close to the end.

Just after the sun came up, I watched how labored his breathing had become. It was as if he was being strangled with every intake. Mother and I knew that death was only a few hours away.

Death or not, my dogs still had to go for their morning walk. I grabbed their leashes.

"I'll only be a minute or two, Mom. I'll make it as fast as I can," I said to her, glancing at my father, who looked so weak and helpless that my heart felt as if it were being torn from my chest.

I walked out of the house and had gotten no further than the end of the block when I noticed that I was standing in front of the house that sat directly behind my mother's home. The woman who lived here had hundreds of ceramic, stone, and pottery angels placed on her porch, in the yard, and hanging from the trees.

All these days and weeks I had been routinely walking my dogs twice a day down this very same sidewalk, not once had I paid any attention to these angels.

Frankly, I surprised myself and realized how immersed I had been in my father's life struggle.

I just stood there looking at those angels and finally blurted out, "If you all are going to come, come on now!"

I walked past her house and cut back through the alleyway into my own backyard.

Oddly, I was struck by the sensation that something or someone was there. I sensed a presence that is hard to describe.

When I looked around, I saw a blue jay on the lawn furniture. I stared at him for a moment and then continued looking around.

I saw another blue jay on the telephone wire. Then another one flew to join him. Then I saw another. And another.

In our part of the country, it is rare to see a blue jay at all. Once a month would be all one could expect. But this . . . was unbelievable.

I bolted into the house and called to my mother.

"Have you ever seen so many blue jays at one time?" I asked my mother, still awestruck.

"Oh sure. They come around every so often," Mother said casually.

I put my arm around her shoulder and walked her to the back porch. "No, Mom. I mean, have you ever seen anything like this?"

I swept my arm across the new vista in our backyard of over thirty majestic blue jays who had congregated and who appeared to be looking right at us.

Mother gasped.

I was still in awe.

The sensations that flooded us both are still hard to describe. We knew we were witnessing the profound. The divine.

Finally, we went back inside the house and went to our various tasks. I took the leashes off my dogs, who normally would have been chasing the blue jays all over the yard but appeared to be as awestruck with the phenomenon of thirty blue jays as Mother and I were.

"Sherry! Come quick!" I heard Mother yell to me from my father's room.

I rushed to her side in time to witness my father taking his last breath.

We both kissed him and held his hand and said a prayer and our good-bye.

I am a nurse, so I knew the protocol. I immediately went to the phone and called the hospice service.

I took the cordless phone to the back porch to make the call and was stunned to find that every single blue jay was gone. I looked all around, even to the neighbor's yard, but there wasn't a one.

I knew even then that the blue jays had been my physical sign that my prayer to the angels and God had been answered. I had asked for my father's release from his pain, and I got it.

During the next week, Mom and I took care of the funeral arrangements, and before I left, I made certain that things were fairly settled at her house for her.

As I drove back to my own home, I was profoundly aware that I had been gone for over two months. My head was filled with all the work I would have to do to get my own life and world back together. At the same time, I was missing my father so much that my breath stung my chest.

I pulled into my driveway and suddenly slammed on the brakes. Sitting on my mailbox was a single majestic blue jay.

My jaw dropped and my heart leapt. My father had heard my heart talking. I knew then he was not gone at all. He was still with me, still able to hear me when I needed him. He and his angel had sent me a blue jay as a sign of love everlasting.

SECTION SIX

Near Death

NEAR DEATH

FIFTEEN YEARS AGO, WHEN I HAD MY NEAR-DEATH EXPErience, there wasn't a great deal of reporting on these occurrences. However, there was enough published that I didn't think I was the first person to go through this, and such reports kept me from believing, well, at least sometimes, that I was crazy.

Each time I have the privilege of speaking on a radio or television show, I almost always receive an email from someone who has also had a near-death experience. In almost every circumstance, that person has told no one about the encounter or they have only shared their story with a very, very trusted person in their life.

I congratulate the people in this section for their courage to share their experiences with us. We all can glean so much information and hope from these stories.

It is not only comforting but also reassuring to know that this life isn't all there is to our experience in the universe. There is a life after this one, and it is going to be even more wonderful than we can imagine.

BURNING ANGEL

AUTHOR'S NOTE: This story was sent to me on March 14, 2006, by a listener when I was on a radio program. There are two distinct parts of this story. One takes place when "Sandra" was six years old. Her near-death experience takes place when she was twenty-seven years old.

AT THE AGE OF SIX, I WAS SAVED BY ANGELS. THEY CAME to me and woke me up sometime during the night.

I felt a tickling of my feet, which woke me up. At first I thought this was my brother, who often tickled my feet to awaken me.

There were two male angels, dressed in robes tied at the waist. The room was filled with a pale blue mist. They were very tall and had no wings, but I knew instantly they were angels.

When I first saw them, I was very scared. However, they were smiling at me.

Three times they repeated, "Do not be afraid. We are here to protect you. Everything is going to be all right."

I didn't say anything to anyone in the family about my visitation. I thought it best to keep such things to myself.

Three days later my dress caught on fire from some trash my mother was burning in the backyard.

I was sitting on the ground playing cars with my brother when I saw the flames. I jumped up and started to run.

I had hair to my shoulders, and bangs as well. As I started to run, my mother could see the flames in my face.

When I reached my mother, she ripped off my clothes and burned her hands in the process.

I went to the emergency room and later had skin grafting. I had first, second, and third degree burns on 35 percent of the right side of my upper body.

118

Eleven years later, my Mom and I were sitting and talking, and I asked her, "Why is it that you never talk about when I got burned?"

"It was just too awful and hard to think about." She paused and then said, "You know, one thing was really strange. The doctor kept saying over and over again, 'I can't believe her hair did not burn.'"

When she said that, I was shocked. I couldn't speak, and tears ran down my cheeks.

"What's wrong?"

"The angels. The angels," I cried.

"What angels?" she asked.

"Before the accident, I was visited by two angels, who told me that they would protect me."

My Mom hugged me and held me for the longest time. We both knew the angels had, indeed, saved my life.

When I was twenty-seven years old and my son was five, I went to sleep one night and experienced what I believe and have been told by a paramedic was most likely a near-death experience.

All of a sudden I was flying through a tunnel with lights, being sucked by a vacuum. The tunnel had black walls and colored lights about the size of a brick randomly placed along the wall. When I got to the end of the tunnel, I stopped, and when I stopped, all of a sudden I felt and realized I was not standing on anything. I was floating.

I could feel a faint mist on my face and body. It was dark but not pitch black.

Then I looked down at my body because I felt really light. When I looked, I could not see my body. I could feel my body. I knew I was whole, I just couldn't see it.

My mind was just as it is right now. I knew everything that was going on. I just did not have control.

Then to my right a bright cloud appeared, and I was very lightly pulled into it.

Then the cloud started to separate in front of me like it was opening up. All of a sudden, there, on the other side of the cloud, was my dad, who was killed in a car accident on September 11, 1963.

At this time, I was able to see my body again.

I ran to my dad and jumped into his arms. Crying and crying, I told him how much I missed him and loved him.

He said, "Turn around."

When I did, there were all these people standing in an oval shape all around me. All of them were friends and family who had died.

I was so, so, so happy. The feeling was indescribable. Love, peace, joy, happiness. It was like nothing I'd ever felt before.

Then a voice from somewhere told me, "You have to go back."

I did not see who was speaking, but I heard him in my head.

I said, "I don't want to go back. My son will be well taken care of. I want to stay here."

"NO! Your work is not done. You have to go back now!"

The next thing I knew, I felt as if a giant hand had grabbed me and pulled me backward into the tunnel.

I was now going back-first through the tunnel with the same speed. I looked over my left shoulder and saw myself lying on the bed. I looked dead.

There was a loud POP and CRACK!

I sat up in bed. I was soaking wet. My hair, my clothes, my bedding were drenched with my own sweat.

Since this experience, I have talked with a friend who is a police officer and with a paramedic, both of whom know about such incidents.

They both think that I had a near-death experience and that I most likely had a fever, died, and came back.

They said I was clinically dead for that time. However, I have no idea how long I was out and up there.

I can certainly say that I am no longer afraid of dying or death. There is life after this life. I am living proof!

IN THE LIGHT

AUTHOR'S NOTE: This story was sent to me by a woman who lives in Salt Lake City, Utah. She was sixty-seven years old at this writing. What struck me was how exact she was about much of her description, as if her near-death experience had happened to her yesterday.

This is the case with those who have near-death experiences. They never forget going to the other side of this life.

I WAS ABOUT THIRTY YEARS OLD WHEN I WENT TO THE hospital for an exam. Suddenly, I became very, very cold. Extremely cold.

Suddenly, I was in a tunnel speeding down it very fast. Ahead of me I could see a white light, and I was racing toward it.

Once I reached the light, I was instantly in the most beautiful garden I had ever seen. I heard you speak of the Crystal City when you were on the radio, and that reminded me of how glittering and gorgeous this garden was.

I remember hearing so many voices. These voices included all of my family members and friends whom I had known and who had now all passed away. It was the most beautiful and peaceful place I have ever been.

Then I heard the voices say, "You have to go back."

"Oh, please! I want to stay here. It's so lovely here," I begged them.

A single voice said, "You must go back. Your work is not finished."

I was incredibly sad and heavy-hearted about leaving. I felt the love of my relatives. I felt the peace of this place. And I knew I would never see such beauty again. It was nearly painful to even think of leaving.

I can't impress upon you how wonderful this place was. Words are just so inadequate in the telling of my experience.

Suddenly, I was no longer in the garden. I was back on earth.

I was calling a nurse while still there in the examination room.

Thank goodness they saw me.

One of them shouted, "She's cold! Please bring warm blankets."

There was a flurry of activity, and several nurses brought blankets. It took a lot of blankets to get me warm again, as you can imagine.

At the time this happened to me, we did not have the Internet or all that we have available to us communication-wise today. I was so desperate to tell my story.

It was so beautiful, but I was afraid that no one would believe me. Things were a lot different then. It is better now. So much better.

I do not like to admit this, but I am sure that my assignment (when I was over there) was to tell my story. That was probably not my only assignment, because now I have four lovely grandchildren. I have so loved watching them grow up, and for them, I'm glad I came back.

Today, knowing that we are not alone is a huge comfort. Knowing that all our loved ones are waiting gives me a great deal of comfort too. I believe that when you die, it is very cold and we leave our bodies and all of our pains or whatever burdens we may have behind us.

Perhaps that is what I needed to know.

I was in a near-fatal car crash four years ago, and I have had to learn how to do everything all over again. I had to learn to walk, talk, eat, and nearly breathe again.

There is one last thing I want to tell you so that you can tell others.

When my dear aunt passed away, it was early in the morning. I felt a presence that morning, and I know now that it was her, letting me know that she was with me. Earlier that summer I had been in California and wanted to see her, but time and schedules didn't work out. Then she died that September. I think she wanted me to know that she wanted to say "good-bye."

I know that it will be only a little while until we will be together again in that most beautiful of all gardens.

NOT SO NEAR DEATH

AUTHOR'S NOTE: In researching near-death experiences by authors such as Dannion Brinkly, "Saved by the Light," Betty J. Eadie, "Embraced by the Light," and others, I have been struck by the fact that many of those who have died and come back also experience heightened psi powers or extrasensory powers. Their intuitions are stronger. Many stay connected to the angels. Some realize they have mediumistic abilities. I have read about those who have turned toward the ministry of one faith or another and have never swayed from that new vocation.

In the following story, this woman was asked by the voice she heard while on the other side to "channel." Although that terminology sounds quite New Age, the ability to prophesy from the divine is very strong in many religions, especially the Christian religion.

I am relating this story just as it was submitted to me, with very few edits, as I have endeavored to do with all the stories in this book.

This is exactly what this woman experienced.

I'VE HAD A NEAR-DEATH EXPERIENCE. IT WAS BECAUSE I was despondent.

I started having a very high fever, and I couldn't get rid of it. I even went to the doctor, but nothing I was given reduced the fever.

I went to bed that night, and I remember actually wondering if I was going to live through the night, it was that severe.

I didn't care if I lived or died.

At some point during the night, I woke up, and in my mind I heard the words, "Do you want to live or die?"

I thought I was dreaming. I even tried to slap my own face, but I couldn't move my arms!

I had heard and read about out-of-body experiences, and my first thought was that I was going through one of these experiences.

I was very frightened at first.

Then I thought that perhaps my angels were talking to me.

I thought about the question. "Do you want to live or die?"

I began to calm down. I realized I did want to die.

Then the pictures and the dialogue started.

I saw myself when I was born and that my parents looked very disappointed.

I was able to ask any question of the angels that I had, and the answers came instantaneously!

It was a very loving and respectful atmosphere.

I was told that I am equal to them. This was very hard for me to believe, since the feeling I had about them was that they were perfection and pretty much indescribable in human language.

I felt as though I was talked into coming back to earth. They used quite a bit of finesse.

"Will you channel?" they asked me.

"Yes," I said immediately.

Then I found myself back in my body in my bed.

After this experience, I felt love for myself for the first time in my life.

I realized that people reacted differently toward me and that they treated me better.

I didn't know much about channeling at the time. I had a friend who told me about it, and she taught me how to keep my mind and heart open to the divine.

I was introduced to my "higher self," and the feeling that I had at the time was "at last." I felt such comfort and peace with the connection to my own divine self.

I don't channel now, but I think that perhaps I actually do when I speak to friends who are seeking advice and words seem to roll out of me. I say things at the time that I don't plan on saying. I honestly don't know where they come from, but they seem to be the right words and the right thing to say.

I have faith and hope today because of this experience I went through. When I die I will welcome it, because it's beautiful.

A CHOICE MADE IN HEAVEN

AUTHOR'S NOTE: This story was sent to me by Ray Wetter. Ray's story is a near-death experience story, though at the time he experienced it, there wasn't really a term for his visit to the afterlife. Again what is interesting to note is that this experience happened nearly thirty years ago and Ray remembers details, like the colors, as if it were yesterday. Such recall is one of the factors that other people who have had near-death experiences all state.

I WAS STATIONED AT RHEIN MAIN AB, FRANKFURT, GER-many. In 1979, I participated in a Re-Forger exercise (return the forces to Germany). On this particular day, we simulated a gas attack and were ordered to don gas masks.

I fell asleep with the gas mask on.

I remember floating up off my cot and through the roof of the tent. I remember being awestruck by the clarity and richness of colors of the sky, flowers, and trees and the deep blue of the sky. I've never seen a sun so bright either.

Also, there was a peacefulness and serenity that I haven't experienced since. I suddenly became aware that I was accompanied by what I assume was an angel. I don't actually recall seeing it, but I did feel it.

In nonverbal communication, I was told that I "had to make a choice."

It wasn't explained to me, but I finally realized that I was choosing life or death. I don't recall an actual "discussion."

I do remember that I knew somehow I was going to get a preview of my life or my death.

I chose life.

The second I made my choice, I suddenly saw my body.

I was on my feet and TSgt. Hughes was behind me with his

arms wrapped around my chest. He was jerking me off my feet trying to get me to breathe.

At that moment, I was back in my body and conscious again.

I ripped the gas mask off and inhaled deeply. I couldn't get enough breath.

I've always wondered if I were meant to do something but haven't known really where to look or search. I know that I have been living a charmed life all my life.

I am married, and my wife and I enjoy a very committed, loving relationship. I have three children, all healthy and mature. I have been blessed with a grandson and good fortune.

I can only thank that angel who gave me the choice in heaven.

SECTION SEVEN

Visions

VISIONS

MANY OF YOU WILL FIND THAT THE STORIES IN THIS section are probably the most fascinating in this book. Thanks to my dear friend, Claire Papin, who so graciously is allowing us to print her story of "Mary's Lullaby" in this book.

Claire's story is more than unique; to me it is astounding. I was raised Catholic and still attend Mass and say my Rosary. As a child, I couldn't imagine anything more incredible than to be visited by the blessed Virgin Mary.

Claire had no religious upbringing and was visited not only by angels but also by "Mother Mary," as Claire calls her, not once, but repeatedly. In speaking with Claire last week, she is still receiving messages from Mother Mary.

The other stories here are remarkable as well, as you will read.

Not only are there reports of visitations from Jesus, but as you read, make note of the various apparel of the angels as they appear to different people. Some people see warrior-type angels in togas and sandals. Others see angels in white robes. Such sightings give credence to the idea that there exist "legions" of angels and that the angels have different "jobs." Some are more warrior-like, doing battle for us. Some are messengers or come to give us strength and hope or to renew our faith.

Whatever the clothing, we are the recipients of divine love at every moment of our lives. And that is blessed indeed.

Mary's Lullaby

AUTHOR'S NOTE: This story was sent to me by Claire Papin, and it is told in her words.

"Peace will stand. It will carry forth in humanity's efforts to aid the planet and humanity itself. We must all remember that we are all one family under God who can choose to participate in the betterment of mankind and the quality of life."

—Mother Mary

MANY EXPERIENCES HAVE LED UP TO THE EVENTS I AM about to share about "Mary's Lullaby." Starting with the night the song first came to me might offer a sense of the overall message from Mother Mary and hope in times of great change.

One night, while curled up on my living room couch reading a book, it was getting late, so I got up to close the blinds and was stopped by a very unusual feeling. I sensed an incredible presence in the room. It was as if I could literally feel a shift of energy, and it brought a tingling sensation. Suddenly, I saw a swirling light begin to encircle me. Then, unbelievably, a beautiful song began pouring from my lips. It was so beautiful that I felt as if I was swept away in its peace and love. This was a song I had never heard before.

After the song ended, a message followed, which I heard both in the room and as an inner voice. "This song is a gift, a blessing, and a prayer," it said. At the same time, like a Technicolor TV screen, a vision flashed before me in which I could see people singing this song in their homes, from many places, and many walks of life. I could see them all at once as if I were looking through the eyes of an angel. The people were surrounded in light, like the light that was encompassing me. I could see past them, through the windows in the house in which we were all standing to the outside, where huge storms were raging. However, inside the house, all the people were in total peace. It was as if they didn't even have a concern about the massive storms. Their faith was strong and there was a joy about them. I could see the love that was beaming on their faces.

The message continued. "This song will be sung in many homes." I somehow knew the song was intended to be recorded and that the right people, place, and time would come together for this to happen. Moments later the vision was gone, and I was left standing in my living room in blissful gratitude. "Oh my God," was all I could say to myself. What I had seen, heard, and felt was beyond words.

As soon as I gathered my composure, I grabbed my tape recorder and quickly sang this song into it so that I would not forget the words and melody of the song. I had never written a song before in my life! This came from an entirely different source than my talent or knowledge. It was from beyond me. A heavenly presence had entered my living room that night, swirled around and through me, brought the nectar of love in song through my lips, and flashed a vision of the future before my eyes that I would later see unfold. A gift had just been given, one that was not only for me but also for others who would benefit from the message this song brings . . . that the peace and love we seek is already within.

A couple of days later, a friend of mine, who is a famous songwriter, was in town. I wasn't quite ready to talk about my experience with people yet, but I did want to share the song. As I sang, he sweetly smiled at me and said, "Claire, that song is a lullaby." I was astounded that the song even had a commercial genre! However, it felt good to know the type of song it was, even though I didn't know why yet.

A few days later, it was time for my weekly prayer meeting with a group of friends. This was a new routine for me that I quickly embraced, even though we had only been gathering for a little over a month. I arrived just in time for the meeting to start. We began with prayer and then we all became silent as we settled into a peaceful state.

After a few moments of quiet, one of the ladies began to speak. She abruptly stated that Mother Mary (the mother of Jesus) was present in the room with us. "She has a message. She says that there is a song, a lullaby, and would that person who was given the song, please sing it."

My heart began to race. This was utterly impossible. I had not spoken about this song or the mysterious way in which it came to me to anyone except my out-of-town friend, who knew none of these people. There is no way this woman could have possibly known about the song or that it was a lullaby.

As these thoughts raced through my mind, I felt the same light energy encircle me as I had experienced the night the song and vision first came.

This energy was powerful but loving. All my misgivings about sharing the song melted.

As I began singing, it felt like a strong pulsation of a heartbeat from the center of the universe to my own chest. Then, in a forward motion, the room was filled with blissful song and prayer. A bright light swirled inside and around me. I was once again in a space of deep peace and love, much like the first night the song came.

When the song was over, I braced myself for what was to come next. My friends' faces were lit up and glowing with smiles, each expressing their similar feeling of the experience.

"Claire, you need to record this song," one of them said.

"Yes, it's so beautiful and peaceful that it should be out there for more people," another said.

With their encouragement pounding in my ears, I shared with them what had happened the night the song first came to me. I told them that I was left with a feeling of knowing that somehow the song was going to be recorded as well. I just didn't know how or when.

We all stood in humble amazement of what just took place. Truly we all believed that we had experienced a visitation from Mother Mary. We were overwhelmed with the beautiful gift of love she had brought to us.

After that night, I experienced a series of unusual synchronistic events that propelled my mission of sharing "Mary's Lullaby" with the world. I am still in awe as I write this.

The following week, a friend, CJ, called from Los Angeles to recommend that I read the book *Mary's Message to the World* by Annie Kirkwood. She didn't know that I had just purchased the book after one of my friends from the meditation meeting had told me about it. Incredibly, she gave me Annie Kirkwood's personal phone number in Dallas. CJ said, "You go to Dallas all the time, don't you? Maybe you should meet her."

Now this was getting more interesting by the day.

How did she even know to call me about this subject out of the blue? I thought.

I took the number, tried calling it, didn't get anyone on the phone, and put it aside. Before I knew it, about a week later, I was on my way to Dallas for some business. While staying at a friend's house, I showed him Kirkwood's book. He was astounded at the timing.

"I just had Annie Kirkwood on my radio talk show last week, I have her number. Would you like it?" he asked.

Even now, I find this incident very interesting. CJ and my friend in Dallas don't know each other. Within a week of receiving the author's number, I got another "universal tap on the shoulder" to call her again.

I didn't waste any time calling Annie. She answered the phone immediately. After briefly sharing how much I enjoyed her book, I explained, "Apparently, people in my life keep giving me your number. Can you tell me why this might keep happening?"

She lovingly said that there was going to be a gathering the following week where an apparition of Mother Mary was expected to occur.

This statement knocked my socks off! Someone was actually expecting to see the Mother of Jesus on a given day at a given time near Dallas. The thought was ludicrous. Impossible.

I had to remind myself that "nothing is impossible with God."

It took a lot of faith and a healthy dose of curiosity for me to alter my schedule and drive to Dallas for this expected apparition. But I did.

About fifty expectant and hopeful people gathered on a clear, sunny day at Joe Pool Lake, just outside of Dallas. After a brief prayer and moment of silence, we saw the sun begin to spin, then, split into two suns. The sight was extraordinary. At first I wanted to deny what I was seeing. However, the vision did not go away, no matter how many times I blinked and looked away. What I saw was very real.

The children who were present saw Mother Mary appear to them. The rest of us experienced a great wave of peace blanketing the area and us. This sense of peace was very similar to the one I'd felt during the time I received the lullaby.

I saw breathtaking waves of rainbow colors spinning out from the sun. Wave after wave of these colorful bands whipped across the sky. It was as if I were in the middle of a fantasy, but it was very real, I assure you.

Frankly, all I could do was stand in awe of the miracles that were taking place before us. For some reason, God had wanted those of us there to receive a more solid knowledge of the presence of love that is continually and eternally here for us. Whether we see it or not, it is always here. To this day, I don't know why I or we as a group were chosen. That is a question I'll ask God when I see him.

All the way home, in prayer, I thanked God for his love and for the opportunity to be present for such a powerful confirmation of the miracles in our lives.

A month later I received a phone call from Kirkwood's husband, Byron. He asked me if I would be interested in being the voice of Mother Mary for the audio version of their book *Mary's Message to the World*. I was thrilled with the invitation. Truly, it was an honor to be asked to again be a part of this blessing to be of service to God.

My bond with Mother Mary, by this time, had changed my life. Over the weeks, Mother Mary had been bringing messages to me in dreams, meditations, and sometimes even while taking walks. They ranged from locutions, which is like a telepathic communication, to luminous visions that would appear in the room.

In particular, there was a time when Mary appeared in a

church accompanied by two angels in all her glowing beauty. I could see a rainbow of light around her and the angels, like a bubble surrounding them. The angels were like the traditional images of angels in Roman times. There were parts of them that were very clear to me and others that faded out. For instance, on one of them, I could see an arm and a side of a body very clearly. He wore robes as in the time of Jesus. I do recall that one was blond and had no facial hair, and I saw only the side of his face. The other angel I couldn't see that well, but I did see dark hair. I could see that they had feet and wore sandals. The togas were short, and I could see their legs. They were definitely masculine in gender at this visitation. I felt as if they were warrior angels or from the Archangel Michael domain.

Interestingly, someone who was there that night at the church took a photograph while the visitation was in progress. I later discovered that the vision I had seen of Mother Mary that night, with the rainbow bubble of light, had shown up in one of the photograph as well.

To be asked to serve by being a voice for Mother Mary and help in sharing her messages in this way was beyond my imaginings. I asked Byron how he knew that I did professional voice-over work.

"We didn't know," was his reply.

When Annie came to the phone, she said, "Mary chose you, Claire, just like she chose me." She continued, "When I asked Mary who was to be her voice, she answered, 'Ask Claire.'"

I accepted in humble gratitude to be a part of sharing the messages from the book.

It was the third day in the studio for the recording of the unabridged version of the book on tape. After several hours of reading, my eyes began to tire, and it was time for a short break. While sipping on water and resting my eyes, I began to feel the strong presence of Mother Mary. She comes with a powerful sense of love that moves through me and around the room much like a window that opens up, bringing a fresh breeze of air filled with the softness of rose petals and the warmth of a mother's loving arms.

The words "It is time to sing the song now," moved through me as a locution, as if lightly tapping me on the shoulder, like a gentle reminder of something already destined to begin its sojourn.

I confided to the producer, who was still sitting in the engineering room, that I had a beautiful song from Mother Mary and asked him if he'd like to hear it.

He said, "Yes."

He quickly loaded a DAT tape. Just as I began to take in a deep breath to begin singing, I could feel, and begin to see, more presences in the room.

This time Mary was joined by Jesus and a bevy of angels, more than I could count. They filled the room with a luminous glow. The walls had disappeared, and the light seemed to go on for eternity.

The vibration or frequency that filled the room from Mary and Jesus and all these angels most definitely affected my physical body. I was completely in bliss. I had not fasted, prayed, or meditated. I was only working that day. I had no preparation in any manner, physical, mental, or even spiritual for what was happening to me. I remember thinking, "This is their idea to use me."

The movement of their frequency through my body as the song began made me think that they were using me as a bridge from their world to my physical world. It is so difficult to describe this experience. It was as if I felt a quickening in every cell of my body grow in resonance of the loving energy in the room. I felt them merging with me. As I began to sing, euphoria and bliss filled my whole being. They were vibrating their love through the sound of my voice.

Once the last word was sung, I could no longer see their presences but could still feel the echo of the blissful state of heaven that had just merged with this world.

I sat in quiet reverence of what had just taken place. As I slowly peered through the window of the engineering room, I could see the producer and engineer gazing into the room, mouths agape, eyes bugged out, and speechless. Although they couldn't see the apparitions, I could tell by their faces that they knew something profound had just happened.

That day, the prophecy Mother Mary had given a month earlier—that the song would be recorded—was fulfilled. "Mary's Lullaby" was added as a theme song to the book on tape and was separately released as a musical meditation tape as well. Thus, "the song could be sung in many homes."

There is one more event that I'm compelled to share, one that speaks to the miracles of the human spirit. A few months after the recording of "Mary's Lullaby," while traveling in the Texas hill country, a friend and I stopped off in a little town called Marble Falls to talk to some realtors. While there, calls were coming in that a huge storm with incredibly strong winds, large hail, and intense lightning was about to arrive. The receptionist was nervously heading for the door to move her car to shelter.

I said to her, "Did you know that you can be in the middle of a raging storm and still be protected?"

"No, I didn't know that. How is it done?" asked the woman. "Through prayer," I replied.

As the woman exited, she smiled in relief, thanked me for the reminder, and said she would be back in a few minutes.

Moments later, the storm struck. The electricity went out in the tiny mobile home office as the building began to rock. Standing in the dark, looking out the window, we witnessed sixty-mile-an-hour winds. No one in the room had ever experienced a storm that fierce in their town. Their fear was nearly tangible and escalating by the second.

"It's okay, everything will be okay." I reassured them.

The others continued to lose confidence in their safety.

"We can stand here looking out the window, talking about how scary it is, or we can do something about it," I said.

"What's that?" they said doubtfully.

"We can pray."

Finally, they commented that it was a good idea. However, they were distracted again by the heightened activity outside the window.

At that moment, I began experiencing the strong inner voice of Mother Mary say, "Claire, sing, and sing now."

"Mother Mary, how am I going to do this when they are so

frightened that I cannot hold their attention?" I asked.

She answered with the same words "Sing, and sing now."

I took a deep breath and asked the others, "Would you like to hear a song?"

To my amazement, they broke their fear-filled trance and replied, "Yes." They quickly gathered some chairs in a circle around me, and "Mary's Lullaby" poured forth while each one of them softened into a calm space.

"That was so peaceful . . . where did that song come from?" asked a lady.

"You could say it came from heaven," I replied.

A moment later, the storm suddenly stopped. Outside, we could see where a tornado had just struck directly across the street from where we were, and the whole town experienced tremendous destruction. National news reported the devastation. And another one of the earlier visions that Mother Mary had brought had manifested itself—the song was inspiring inner peace as storms raged outside.

I've been sharing these experiences at gatherings around the country. I have seen the awesome transformation that can occur when we open our minds to the miracles that happen daily. Our hearts reawaken, and our true spirit of limitlessness comes forth, no matter the circumstances in life. Mother Mary has shared this message: "Peace will stand. It will carry forth in humanity's efforts to aid the planet and humanity itself. We must all remember that we are all one family under God, and members of the human race who can choose to participate in contributing to the betterment of mankind and the quality of life."

AUTHOR'S NOTE: When I interviewed Claire, I was curious if she had ever heard about the vision of Our Lady of Fatima, at which time the sun was reported to have spun in gyrating circles, then split in two and spewed bands of sparkling colors across the sky. Claire told me she had never been raised in any religion at all. She had been once to a Catholic church as a child, but she had never heard about this vision or any vision of Mother Mary. She also did not know that Catholics call Mary the Mother of Jesus, the "Blessed Virgin." Claire had no prior training or indoctrination into any kind of reports of Mary's visitations around the world. Claire knew only what she experienced. As we are coming to understand, her visitation is not unique, but it is very special. Claire is just one example of the infusion of messages and information coming to our lives from heavenly beings, angels, and loving spirits from heaven, or rather the other side of our plane of existence here on earth.

It is also interesting to note that Claire went back to Joe Lake Pool outside Dallas much later and experienced a second visitation from Mother Mary along with fifty to sixty other witnesses.

The Path of Miracles

AUTHOR'S NOTE: This life-altering miracle story is from Claire Papin. It is written in her words.

THE FOLLOWING IS A DREAM I EXPERIENCED A FEW years ago.

In the dream, I was driving down the freeways of Los Angeles on a beautiful sunny California day. I ended up at a small strip of a white sandy beach with crystal blue waters and about twenty or so people romping and having fun. They didn't seem to notice me standing there, almost as if I was invisible. I was dressed in business attire: a dark blue dress, hose, and dress shoes. I approached the shoreline, stopped, and looked down at my right hand, and in it was a Miraculous Medal.

The thought came to me that I needed to throw it into the ocean, but I didn't know if it would make it that far. I drew my hand back as far as I could, then gave a forward thrust with all my might and threw it into the water. All of a sudden an explosion of light burst before me. I didn't know exactly what was happening, but I knew it was something wonderful.

I remember thinking when I awoke, "Wow, what was that?" It had the feeling of having a divine origin of some kind and left me with a strong sense of hope.

It was time to get dressed and head out to my new job anchoring traffic on Houston's news station KTRH. It was my first time to do live broadcast radio, and I was pretty nervous. I sprang out of bed, dressed, and headed out the door.

My mother's house was on the way, and as it turned out, there was plenty of extra time, so I decided to make a quick stop off at her place to say hello.

After our hugs, she mentioned that she had found something

on the floor in a used bookstore and somehow knew that she was supposed to give it to me. As she placed it in my right hand, I looked down and noticed that it was a Miraculous Medal.

"Mom, this is amazing, I just had a dream this morning where a Miraculous Medal showed up in my right hand."

"Really?"

"Yes. I think that's very strange. But good strange. Well, I gotta go. I'll tell you more about it later," I said.

She gave me a big kiss on the cheek and sent me off with a snack for later.

As I walked into the studio, there was an older man with a kind-looking face, sitting in a wheelchair at a long, white counter with a microphone in front of him, delivering the latest traffic report on the air. A moment later, he removed his headphones and smiled as he introduced himself.

"Hi, I'm Steve. You must be Claire."

Before I could open my mouth, a thought shot through my head, "So how long do you think you're going to be in that wheelchair?"

I gasped at such a confrontational thought, not being a very confrontational person, I couldn't imagine myself even thinking such a pointed question.

"Y . . . Yes, I'm Claire. Very nice to meet you," I finally got the words out.

And then the most extraordinary thing happened. He answered my unspoken question as he pointed to his wheelchair, saying, "Ohhh, you mean this?"

He had actually heard my thought. I silently squirmed. "Uh . . . yes, that." (I gestured toward his chair.)

Now you're probably asking yourself, "Why would she just answer him as if she really asked the question out loud?" Well, by this point in my journey, there have already been a number of unexplainable events I've been party to. I decided not to fight it and to go with the flow, curiously following the trail of where this was leading.

He quite matter-of-factly shared, "I've been in this chair almost six months now. My doctor says that my condition is only going to get worse because my legs have degenerated too much to ever recover and walk again. The tough part has been to learn to emotionally adjust to the situation."

My heart sank and went into full overdrive compassion for this sweet spirit of a man. Before I could stop myself, words began to pour from my mouth, "I don't believe that you have to be in that wheelchair the rest of your life. There's so much you can do for your health. There are all kinds of holistic methods out there to support you, and besides that . . . I believe in miracles!"

Suddenly, I stopped, realizing my mouth had run away with my thought. In my head, I berated myself. *Uhhhh! Claire, what are you doing? You don't have a right to get this man's hopes up about something like that.*

He looked at me with a somewhat startled but grateful look on his face, almost like he came to a realization that he was in the presence of a close family member to whom he could confide.

I realized I had already gone past the point of no return in "coming out" with where I thought this conversation might be going at this point.

"Steve, may I share with you an example of a miracle?"

He nodded, intrigued.

"Let me tell you about a dream I had just last night."

I told him about the dream of the Miraculous Medal and how my mother had just handed me a Miraculous Medal on my way into the studio. Steve stayed glued to every word.

Then I asked, "Do you know the story of the Miraculous Medal?"

"No, I don't" he replied.

"Well, I'm not Catholic, but I've heard the story from a nun that I recently met. The story goes like this. In the 1800s, I think it was around 1856, there was a young woman who lived in France named Catherine Laboret who had an apparitional visit from Mother Mary, the mother of Jesus. Mary asked her to strike or have designed and formed, a medal of the vision that Catherine had been given of her. Then Catherine was to distribute the medals to the people because there was about to be a great challenge. Mary said that the medals were a gift for the people and were to be thought of as a symbol of a prayer.

"Shortly after that, Catherine convinced a priest to help her get the vision struck onto a medal and, consequently, was able to get the medals out to the people of that area.

"Within months, the bubonic plague hit Europe. Everyone who had received the medal did not perish from the plague.

"Everyone who got the plague but later received a medal also did not perish from the plague.

"Thus the medal's name: Miraculous Medal."

Steve was staring at me, dumbfounded but enthralled with the story.

"Steve, I think the idea that Mother Mary was trying to convey was that, with intention and prayer, there's always hope for a miracle."

He looked at me with tear-filled eyes while I pulled the Miraculous Medal out of my pocket. "It's so good to know that someone cares," he said.

"Steve, we all care. It's just that some of us have forgotten we care, and it gets covered up by the forgetfulness, but the care is still there," I replied.

Tears began to roll down his face. I reached for his hand and gently placed the medal into his palm. I silently said a very quick prayer for him.

We smiled at each other with an unspoken gratitude. The moment felt almost timeless.

It was almost time for my shift to start, so we hugged and said our good-byes.

I can remember taking my seat with my headphones in my hands, about to go on the air, thinking how there really are no strangers in this world and how close we all really are to one another. As I placed my headphones over my ears, I could hear my producer letting me know I had fifteen seconds. I began to chuckle to myself as I noticed I wasn't as nervous as I thought I'd be.

Two days later, I received a phone call from a friend of mine, Reverend Lucas. He mentioned that he had some business in Los Angeles relating to his work with the homeless and remembered that I used to live there. He thought I might be able to recommend a place for him to stay.

Reverend Lucas and I had spent a good amount of time together working with the homeless, from serving meals to offering healing services in his church. There were times when I would witness people moving beyond living on the streets, where Reverend Lucas was able to help them find steady employment and support them by giving them a place to stay.

As I shared some possible options on some hotels in the area, Reverend Lucas asked if I might be able to go with him. He told me that my other two friends, Marylyn and Rhonda, were also going. He thought I might be able to be of some help.

As I explained that I had only just begun a new job and that I wasn't sure if I would be able to come up with the ticket money so soon, I remembered the dream I had only two days before where I was in Los Angeles.

Then he said that Marylyn had an extra frequent flyer ticket that I could use.

There must be some reason that I need to go on this trip, I thought to myself.

How could I say no? It was too synchronistic to ignore.

"Okay, Reverend Lucas, just let me know the details, and I'll be there."

I decided to bring a Miraculous Medal with me, just in case I ended up at an ocean while we were there.

It was a beautiful, sunny California day. We arrived without a hitch and were unloading our luggage into our hotel rooms. Marylyn, Rhonda, and I were sharing a room, while Reverend Lucas had a room a few doors down. The first order of business was dinner, then off to work to go over our plans for the business meetings scheduled over the next couple of days.

I discovered that morning that we would be going to a meeting in Malibu at a restaurant called the Sand Castle. Even though Malibu is mostly cliffs and doesn't quite match the kind of beach I had in my dream, I decided to bring a Miraculous Medal with me anyway.

We were being seated when I looked out the window ahead and saw a small strip of a white sandy beach right outside the restaurant's back door. There were people romping and having fun in full beach attire, and I could see beautiful, crystal blue waves rise up from the ocean. As the waitress was handing us our menus, I asked how I might be able to slip outside to the beach for a moment.

She pointed out where the back door was and said, "You know, it's pretty strange. This is the first time I've ever seen this many people this time of year out there on the beach."

I pulled a Miraculous Medal out of my purse, excused myself, and then headed straight for the back door.

As I stepped onto the sand, I realized I was so caught up in the moment of the likeness of this beach and setting to my dream that I completely forgot that I was wearing high-heeled shoes and hose.

However, it didn't matter, I told myself. I had come all this way, and I was going for the ocean.

As I walked toward the shoreline, it didn't even seem to phase the onlookers that I was there, dressed in business attire.

I got as close to the water as I could and stopped watching the ebb and flow of the waves. "If I get any closer, the water will wash over my shoes and stocking feet. If I don't get close enough, I don't know if the medal will reach."

I drew my hand back as far as I could, then gave a forward thrust with all my might and threw the medal into the water. A giant wave reached up just at that moment and snatched the medal right in midflight. I stood in awe at the timing and then began to notice my body vibrating, like electricity moving through me from head to toe. I knew something wonderful was happening, but I didn't know what.

When we got back to Houston and I returned to work, it happened to be on the same day that Steve was working the shift before me. He only worked on weekends because he had another job during the week. I made it to work just moments before my time to go on the air, and I quickly raced into the studio.

Steve had already kindly plugged my headphones in and

waited for my entrance. I motioned a thankful wave as I hastily positioned myself for my first feed. A moment later, I was finished with my on-air report. I looked up at Steve to thank him and noticed something different. There was no wheelchair.

There was no wheel chair!

Steve was standing up on his own two feet next to a cane that was leaning on the wall close by.

I looked at him in astonishment. "Steve, what happened?"

He said, "I just got mad at that chair and decided to get up and walk."

"Oh my!" I said. "That's WONDERFUL. When did this happen?"

"Just a couple of days ago," he said.

I was in absolute awe of this incredible miracle that took place.

He looked at me very seriously. "Who are you? After meeting you, my life has changed."

"Steve, I'm you," I said. "We are all the same. We are all one. It was YOU who decided to get up out of that chair and walk, with just a mustard seed of faith."

FOUR ANGELS FOR DAVID

WHEN I WAS ABOUT NINE YEARS OLD, I NEEDED TO climb up a rock from a beach where I was playing with my friend.

The rock was about twenty-five to thirty feet high. For a young boy, that rock and cliff area was pretty intimidating. I was afraid that if I couldn't climb that rock, I'd never get back to my family. I'd never see home again. A thousand dire thoughts went through my head. A young imagination is a fairly strong force.

I started to cry. Then I prayed for help.

Just then, about twenty feet in front of me and about three feet above me, I saw a group of four beings. They did not have wings, but I thought them to be angels. At least that's what I felt in my heart and mind.

They were dressed in long robes, all in earth-tone colors. I didn't see their mouths move, but in my mind, I heard them tell me not to worry.

"We will help you get off the cliff."

I looked up at the steep cliff wall.

"How? It's impossible!" I said.

"You just turn around," they said and told me what to do.

I did just as they instructed.

I started to climb up.

Then, as I was climbing, I felt a strong hand on my back as I made my way to the top.

When I reached the top and was finally safe, I wanted to thank them, but they were gone. I looked in every direction, but they had vanished.

"Thank you, anyway. Whoever you are! You saved me!"

A few days later, I went back and looked at the same cliff. I was stunned to realize what I had managed to climb. It was incredibly high and very difficult. It now looked like there wasn't a foothold to be seen. I knew then that I'd never be able to do it again. I had known it was impossible the first time, and I was right!

I will never forget those robed beings.

I won't forget to continue to thank them for helping me that day either.

JESUS ON THE HILL

AUTHOR'S NOTE: This story was given to me by Philip Janquart. In his mother's life, there were two incidents of angelic intervention. In both cases her role as a mother was challenged.

PHILIP'S MOTHER, KATHRYN, WAS GIVING BIRTH TO HIS younger sister, Melissa. It was a difficult birth and involved a great deal of pain. Over the many hours of labor, Kathryn envisioned herself climbing a very high hill, and once she reached the top of the hill, the pain would subside. She would then venture down the other side of the hill pain free. This process went on for a very long time.

As the labor continued, the pain became so intense that it was unbearable. She looked over to Philip's father, Philip Sr., and said to him, "I just can't do it anymore."

Suddenly, her body went completely limp.

At that moment, she had been climbing the highest hill of all. When she reached the very top, she saw Jesus. He reached out his hand to her and said, "Yes, you can do it. Here, I'll help you." She reached out her hand to Jesus, and he pulled her up the mountainside. Suddenly she was filled with strength. She was able to deal with the pain.

Melissa was born healthy and robust. There were no complications during the rest of the delivery.

To this day, Kathryn swears that her experience was not a vision, but a real, physical interaction. She states that she does not remember seeing Jesus's face, but she does remember seeing his hair. He wore a long, white robe and sandals. She also distinctly remembers his hand and what it felt like to touch his flesh. She always says, "That's what happened. It was real, and no one will ever tell me any different."

A few years later, Philip's brother, Travis, was born. However, Travis, unlike Melissa, was not healthy. He had cancer. For two years, the tiny baby battled the disease. The entire family prayed for divine intervention, but it never came.

For two years Travis's cancer had been spreading out of control. It covered all but a very small portion of his internal organs. It appeared in lumps under his skin on his head, hands, arms, and legs. All of the doctors told the family that Travis was probably not going to live.

Month after month the family lived through CAT scan after CAT scan that revealed the progressive, onward march of the deadly disease. Truly, it looked as if the doctors were right and Travis's lifespan would be short.

Despondent and nearly out of hope, Kathryn did not know where to turn.

Finally, she found solace in a retreat center associated with her church. It was there that she found the strength to give Travis over to God. She spent a weekend in prayer and meditation delving deep into her own soul.

"I love him more than anything, God," she said, sobbing, through a prayer. "But if you take him, I understand."

On the drive home from the retreat center, Kathryn heard a voice that she believes was from an angel, if not from Jesus himself.

"It's over. Your son's purpose has been fulfilled," the divine voice said.

At first she didn't believe the voice and even doubted it. It was too fantastical to imagine that it was actually happening. The voice did not come from inside her head. It was not her intuition. It was not her conscience. It was a male's voice, and he conveyed the same kind of strength and power that she remembered when she had met Jesus on the hill. For this reason, she often wonders if it was Jesus. However, this time she did not see Jesus as she had during Melissa's birth.

By the time Kathryn reached home, she realized that her prayer had been answered and this was the answer. This angel or messenger had been sent to give her exactly this message.

When Kathryn arrived at her house, she found her husband,

Philip Sr., there, which was unusual because she had expected him to be at work. Philip explained that he had felt ill that day and had decided to come home and be with Travis. However, the most interesting thing had happened.

"Something is different with Travis today," he said.

"What do you mean?"

"He has more energy and is clearly not in pain. And he seems much happier," Philip Sr. said.

Kathryn went over to Travis and picked him up. She looked into his face. The baby smiled up at her. She felt in her heart that she was looking into the face of an angel. At that moment, she knew. She knew that a real angel had spoken to her and that her prayer to God had been answered.

A couple of weeks later, it was time for Travis's scheduled CAT scan. The doctor was amazed as he explained to Kathryn and Philip Sr. that Travis's cancer had inexplicably halted. For the first time since Travis's birth, the cancer had not progressed.

"I don't understand how this is possible," the doctor said.

"I do," Kathryn said. "It's a miracle. God's miracle."

"Sometimes when babies are born with cancer, their immune systems are able to fight the disease off somehow. We don't know how this happens, but it can."

"How often does this happen?" Kathryn asked.

"It's rare," the doctor replied.

"How rare?" Philip Sr. pressed.

"Very."

Because the doctor was not so sure about the results of the tests and what he was actually seeing, he scheduled a CAT scan in three weeks' time.

The family returned to the hospital for yet another CAT scan. This time the tests revealed that the cancer had regressed. With each passing day, Travis grew stronger. The family became more convinced that it was no coincidence that the cancer regression coincided exactly with the timing of Kathryn's prayer in which she put Travis's life in God's hands and relinquished her mother's control.

Within two months the cancer was completely gone.

Travis grew to be an all-state defensive and offense lineman for his high school football team. He is married, and he and his wife own and operate their own landscaping company. They have just given birth to their first child, a happy and healthy miracle of God.

PATRICIA'S ANGEL VOICE

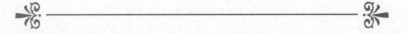

AUTHOR'S NOTE: This story was submitted by Patricia R. Moore-Donley.

PATRICIA WAS FOURTEEN YEARS OLD WHEN SHE HAD HER first angel intervention. She and her younger sister, Phoebe, were sunbathing down by the creek behind their parents' home in Tremont City, Ohio. This was a particularly beautiful secluded area with a tree-lined path that ran down a hill to the creek. It was the kind of place that would give solace to anyone seeking a meditative moment in nature. Patricia and Phoebe simply had fun on their minds, and basking in the sun seemed to fit that bill.

They placed a blanket on the ground and stretched out. Looking up at the azure blue sky filled with clouds scudding their path across the heavens, they talked about everything young girls share with each other.

Suddenly, they both heard a cracking and popping noise.

Patricia bolted upright. "Did you hear that?"

"Yeah."

They both looked around to the trees and shrubbery behind them. "Do you think someone is watching us?" Patricia asked.

They scoured the area with their eyes, but saw no other movements of any kind.

"Maybe it was just a rabbit or something darting through the thicket," Patricia said.

"Let's hope."

Uneasily, they both laid back down.

CRRRRRRRACKKKKKKK!

This time the noise was twice as loud as the first time. Phoebe jumped to her feet. "Trish. This is not good!"

She raced up to the top of the hill, looking for the origin of the noise.

The barn was located at the top of the hill, so it made sense that such a loud noise could be from there. The barn used to be an old carriage house, and behind the barn was a corral. Occasionally, the horses would push down the boards of the fence and romp around town and chase the townsfolk. It was always a mess if one of the horses got out. It stood to reason Phoebe would think that the noise was similar to one of the horses knocking at the fence.

Patricia cupped her hands around her mouth and yelled, "Is it coming from our barn?"

"No!" Phoebe yelled back and began walking back to the blanket.

Patricia lay back down and stared up at the sky and the large canopy of limbs and leaves provided by the Sycamore tree above her.

Suddenly, Patricia realized just where the cracking and popping noise was coming from.

The huge Sycamore tree was falling straight to the ground. In seconds, it would land on her.

In that nano-moment, Patricia was frozen with fear. She sensed she would be killed. She didn't think. She simply watched the enormous tree descend.

From out of nowhere, a very deep, booming male voice yelled loud enough to echo from earth to kingdom come, "ROLL!"

Patricia didn't think to ask who was talking or where he came from.

She did just as the voice commanded.

She rolled.

She rolled three times. The tree landed exactly on the spot where Patricia had been lying on the blanket.

Again, Patricia was frozen. She couldn't take her eyes off the fallen tree.

Phoebe came running to her. "Are you all right? You could have been killed!"

Patricia got up slowly and looked around to the trees, the

creek, the hill, and on farther to where the family barn sat. She didn't see anyone. Where was the man who yelled at her?

"Did you hear that voice?" Patricia asked Phoebe.

"What voice?"

"You didn't hear that loud voice? Telling me to roll?"

"No."

"You had to have heard it. It saved my life!"

"Honest, Trish, I didn't hear anyone or anything."

In minutes, half the family was running toward them. Patricia's mother was the first to come down the hill. The fallen tree had made such a horribly loud noise that even the old man from down the street at the garage came running.

To this day, Patricia marvels that the sound of that voice was twice as loud as the thunderous noise the fallen Sycamore made. Yet she is the only one who heard the voice of her angel.

MOTHER AND THE ANGEL

AUTHOR'S NOTE: This story was submitted by Patricia J. Smith.

MY MOTHER PASSED AWAY IN FEBRUARY 1997. I CARED for her along with my father for the last three months of her life, at home. I had a guardian angel pin that I had received from my boss while working at a hospital. I thought it would give her some comfort.

Every night after her death, I prayed that she made it to heaven. I also asked for a sign. As a human being, I was looking for a bolt of lightning, a white dove, or a rainbow—something like that. But two months later I received a sign I will never forget!

I had been awakened in the middle of the night with a runny nose and sinus congestion. It was impossible to get comfortable. I was now wide awake and unable to fall back asleep. As I lay there, in my totally darkened room, a bright, glowing form appeared, starting from the bottom going upward until the form was complete. It was a solid, white, glowing entity that looked like an angel. Not the typical angel you see in books. It must have stood ten feet tall, had very large wings, a head that seemed too small for its body, no facial features, no feet.

It was very still and very peaceful. It didn't speak, but it gave me a sense of love and peace. I rubbed my eyes, thinking I was seeing something. I even looked to another part of the room and returned my eyes to where I had seen it, and it appeared again.

It was at that moment I knew it was a sign directly from God that Mother had arrived at her destination! I don't know how long it stayed there, but it was so beautiful. The glow didn't even hurt my eyes. I went back to sleep and awoke the next morning without the sniffles, and I could clearly see the image of that angel in my head. Nine years later, I can still see it as though it were a painting on my heart. It's really true. God does hear our prayers!

ANGEL ON THE LAND ROVER

AUTHOR'S NOTE: This story was sent to me by Reverend Dr. Richard Stewart. This story took place in the autumn of 1987.

I BOUGHT A LAND ROVER SHORT WHEELBASE MILITARY Lightweight at the NATO Air Force base at Ramstein. This vehicle was specially made to be extra light so it could be dropped out of cargo planes, attached to a platform with parachutes. It was a funny-looking Jeep-type vehicle. I added modifications that the military did not add to make the vehicle more highway friendly, as this vehicle was designed to be an off-road vehicle.

I used to get a lot of funny looks as I drove my British Lightweight Land Rover. One Friday night, I set out to drive from my office in Boston down to my father's home in Fairfield, Connecticut, to visit with the family. Overall, it's a three-hour trip. About ten miles into the state of Connecticut, a bright, shiny new Chevy pickup truck passed me, with its driver talking on his car phone.

All of a sudden, the pickup truck burst into flames about a quarter mile ahead of me. The truck pulled over into the breakdown lane in a big hurry.

I pulled up behind it and jumped out, went to the back door of my Rover, and pulled out two, ten-pound fire extinguishers, one a CO_2 and the other a dry chemical.

I ran up and sprayed the extinguishers under the engine compartment and was able to temporarily put out the fire.

The driver was panicked because he had electric door locks, and the wiring harness was fried so he couldn't get out of his new truck. I yelled at him to turn the other way and smashed his window with one of the extinguishers.

I reached in, grabbed the driver, and yanked him out.

Right then the truck burst into flames again.

The driver and I ran to a hillside beyond the emergency breakdown lane.

A state trooper just happened to be passing by as I was smashing the window and pulling the man out of his truck. He called for the fire department, and then he went to a highway break to turn around. The trooper pulled up to check if everyone was out of the pickup, while the truck was now fully engulfed in flames.

The fire department showed up and put out the fire. The police and firefighters were speaking with the driver of the pickup.

My feet felt like they were nailed to the ground. I just stood and watched the proceedings, as my vehicle was surrounded by all kinds of apparatus. I had to wait until all of this equipment left so I could proceed on my way.

Finally, a ramp bed tow truck pulled up to take away the burnt truck. Right then I was nudged forward on the back of my left shoulder. Then there was this voice that told me, "Ask him where he is going . . ."

I wasn't sure if that command was for me, so I ignored it.

Again, I was pushed from behind, on the rear of my left shoulder.

I turned around with a clenched fist only to see that there was no one there!

Again, I was pushed, and again I was told to "ask him where he is going."

Again I turned around to see who had now nudged me three times and told me to ask the driver where he was going.

I was a wee bit heated that some wise guy thought he could be funny. I turned around again, and once again, I saw no one!

Just then the state trooper came and began asking questions, wanting a statement from both of us.

"No problem." I told him what I saw and what I did.

He then asked the owner of the pickup his story.

The owner spoke to the trooper as the pickup was being dragged up on the flat bed of the tow truck.

The trooper left us, and once again I was pushed from behind on my left shoulder.

This time the voice said, "Ask Paul where he was going."

I turned around with clenched fist ready to deck someone, and once again, there was no one there.

I spun completely around looking for anyone who could have pushed me.

I asked the owner of the pickup, "Did you see who shoved me?"

"No," he answered.

I asked, "Is your name Paul?"

He turned and looked at me with great big eyes. "How did you know my name? I didn't tell you."

I then asked him, "Where were you going tonight?"

Paul responded, "Huh?"

"Where were you going tonight?" I asked again.

With bugged eyes, he said, "I'm headed to Fairfield, Connecticut."

"Where in Fairfield?" I asked.

He told me the location.

"That's about a mile and a half from where I'm going. When that tow truck takes away your pickup, why don't you get in with me, and I'll take you to where you are going since we are going to the same town."

"You're really going to Fairfield?" Paul asked.

"Yes. I'm going to Southport, part of Fairfield, which is only a mile or so from where you are going. My dad's house is about half a mile into Southport."

Paul's pickup was hauled away, and we climbed into my jeep. A very vibrant discussion then began between the two of us. He was totally dumbfounded that the person who saved his life by pulling him out of his burning truck was going to the same town, and nearby the same part of town, as he was headed.

Being a pastor at that time, I began speaking to Paul about angels, God, and being born again. He asked me if I was ordained and with whom.

I told him I held ordination with several organizations and then listed them, ending with the Assembly of God denomination.

He then burst forth that his mother was an Assembly of God pastor and that she had been trying to get him saved for years.

I asked him his mother's name, and he told me.

I was astonished to discover that I knew his mother.

By this time, Paul was getting really "buggy."

"Paul, I don't think it's a coincidence that I was the one who stopped to help you. And then to take you to your final destination."

Paul was really beginning to freak out.

For the rest of the hour and a half trip, I rambled on about the Bible, angels, and weird experiences.

We finally arrived at his friend's house. I asked him if he would allow me to pray with him before we departed each other's company. Paul agreed.

We got out of the Land Rover. I prayed over him and anointed him with some oil, and then he and I prayed vivaciously together. I led Paul in a prayer, where he repeated after me my words to him.

I shook his hand and said, "If you need, I can give you a ride back to Boston on Sunday. I can put you on a train or bus in Boston back to Maine."

"I appreciate your offer, but no. I'll be all right now that I'm here," he said.

I got into my Land Rover and backed out of the driveway. I started down the street.

Paul ran out of the driveway yelling at me.

I stopped and looked out my window.

"Who are you?" Paul yelled.

I pulled on my emergency brake and stepped out of the vehicle. "I'm a guy just like you, I pull my pants on one leg at a time."

Paul was still running toward me. "What's your name?" he yelled.

"It doesn't really matter," I said.

Paul then burst into tears and ran up to me and hugged me like a baby.

"I don't cry at anything," he said. "But there is something special about you. By the way, there is an angel flying above you."

I wiped Paul's face and said, "Everything is going to be all right. God had you in his hands."

"It's true. I don't know why I feel this," he said and then kissed me on my cheek.

He walked back to his friend's driveway.

I hopped back into my jeep and began to pull away again.

Again Paul ran back toward me, asking once again, "Who are you? You never told me your name."

I stuck my head out my window and said, "My name is Richard."

"Richard, who are you?"

I just waved and pulled away.

I spent the weekend with my dad and two younger brothers. Sunday afternoon I packed up and headed back to Boston.

Cresting the same hill where Paul's truck had burst into flames, there he was again, having a temper tantrum on the side of the highway with two other people with a car hood opened up and steam pouring out.

I pulled over and told Paul to stop with the temper tantrum. "Get into my truck."

Paul ran up and hugged and kissed me. He got into the passenger's seat. His two friends stood with mouths hanging wide open in disbelief.

One of them walked up to me and said, "We didn't believe Paul about the kind stranger bringing him home after his truck burned up. Now we know it must be true."

I looked under the hood of Paul's friend's car.

It was a ruptured hose. No big deal.

"There's a gas station with all kinds of parts just down the road. Sit tight, and I'll be right back."

I bought a new hose, antifreeze, and water. I returned to the scene and replaced the hose, poured in the antifreeze and water. "You're all set now," I said.

They were all dumbfounded and grateful for my generosity.

I noticed the Connecticut license plates on Paul's friend's car.

"Are you going to drive Paul all the way to Lewiston, Maine?"

"Yes," the woman answered. We'll spend the night and come right back to Connecticut tomorrow morning."

"I think it might be better if Paul continues on with me and lets you two ladies go back home to Fairfield."

"If you don't mind taking me to the bus in Boston, Richard, that would be great."

"I don't mind at all."

Paul said good-bye to the ladies and got in my truck.

The lady driver rolled down her window and said to me, "Who are you? You must be the same person who picked up Paul the other night. You had such a profound affect on Paul Friday night. He was so very different all weekend long."

I gave the ladies instructions on how to turn around at the next exit. Then I climbed into my jeep.

As Paul and I were pulling away, the two women were pointing above my jeep screaming something about an angel.

"An angel! There's an angel over your Land Rover!" they yelled.

I took Paul to downtown Boston and put him on a bus back to Maine. I gave Paul my business card right before he left.

A week later I received two tickets and two coupons for a free meal at Paul's restaurant in Lewiston, Maine. About fourteen months later, I went to Lewiston for my free meal.

I arrived on a Friday night at the final call for dinner. Paul was having a birthday party for his ailing mother.

When I walked into the restaurant, Paul spotted me from the farthest corner, and he ran across two dining rooms. He ran right up to me and threw his arms around me and kissed me on both sides of my face.

The entire restaurant suddenly went completely hushed. You could have heard a pin drop.

"I'm so glad you came. It's funny your timing, because it's my mother's birthday and my family is celebrating in the back corner. Mother will be so glad to meet you. I've told her all about you and the angel that flies over your jeep.

Paul ushered me back to where his family was celebrating.

When I came into view of his mother, her eyes got very wide, and she started crying. She remembered when we had first met.

I was at a pastor's conference at her church about an hour

northeast of Lewiston, approximately a year before I met Paul in his burning truck.

Paul's mother told everyone how I had saved a little girl's life at her church when I was there for the conference. She went on to say that she wasn't a bit surprised that it was I who had pulled Paul out of his burning truck and just happened to be going to the same town he was going to.

I was the honored guest that night along with Paul's mother. I was then told under no uncertain terms that I would spend the night at Paul's mother's house.

His mother said that I had a "message from God" to bring forth to her congregation that Sunday morning. She wanted me to stay to deliver that message.

God had burdened me with a message from his heart for a couple of weeks, but I didn't know if I would have the chance to preach it or just file it away for a rainy day.

That Sunday morning, I preached what God had put into my heart, plus I told the story of meeting Paul and the burning truck.

I received many hugs from numerous strangers at Paul's mother's church. After services, we went out to lunch. After lunch I had to bid everyone farewell and head back to Boston.

Paul's mother hugged me and slipped a check and some cash into my hand.

Mother said to me, "I am so grateful to God for you, because you had such a profound affect on my son, Paul, that night you picked him up. He's not been the same. Plus your presence here this weekend has touched him once again. Surely you have God in you and with you. I am so grateful for your life."

I parted ways with Paul, his mother, and their friends and congregation members.

Two weeks later I received a call from Paul that his mother's health had taken a dramatic turn for the worse, and she had passed away. I drove one last time to Maine to be a part of the funeral proceedings.

When I got there, everyone at the funeral told me that Paul's mother wanted me to know that she had seen the angel that flew over my Land Rover.

She had asked Paul to make sure that I was at the funeral, and she told him that she had seen the angel.

TELEVISION ANGELS

AUTHOR'S NOTE: the following story is truly extraordinary. Though I have exchanged several emails with the author of this piece, he chooses to remain anonymous. I am grateful to him for his submission to this book. "Your work is important," he says. I will refer to him in this story as George Dawson.

IN 1998 GEORGE'S WIFE PASSED AWAY FROM IBC BREAST cancer. No matter how much a person believes that they are prepared for the death of a spouse, the reality of the enormity of the situation when it hits is devastating. Understandably, George was overwhelmed with grief and loss.

In those days following the funeral, when he was at home, everything about his surroundings reminded him of his beloved wife. Grief has a tendency to render a person zombie-like. George was no exception.

About a week after the funeral, George woke up in the morning and heard the television in the living room. There was no question in his mind that he had turned the television off. As there was no one living in the house except himself, there was no reason for the television to suddenly come on.

Getting out of bed, he put on his robe and went to the living room. What he saw as he entered the room caused him to stand stock still.

Sitting on the daybed where his wife had passed away were two young women. They were complete strangers. One was about eighteen years old, and the other was about twenty years old. They were both slim and pretty and had brown, medium-length hair. Both of them were dressed in jeans.

They said nothing to him and kept their eyes on the television.

George glanced at the television and thought it was very odd that the program that they were watching was only in black and white.

He looked back at the young women, but still, they never took their eyes from the television. He started walking toward them, and the younger one of the two glanced at him out of the corner of her eye.

At that moment, George experienced an incredible rush of emotion. He had the feeling of overwhelming, unconditional love and pure bliss. It was a feeling that he had never experienced in his life to that point. The feeling was absolutely euphoric.

As the feeling completely engulfed him and before he had a chance to say anything to either of the two young women, George felt as if he were being pulled back into his bedroom.

Awake again in his bed, he got up from the bed and went into the living room to see if the young women were still there. However, they had vanished. The television was off.

To this day, George does not know if what he experienced was a dream or if his soul was traveling or if he had been given a vision and does not remember walking back into the bedroom. One thing he does know is that the experience is one he will never forget. For him, the incident was incredibly clear and very real.

George also believes that these two women were sent to him as a sign and a message that his wife is at peace in heaven.

For those who have been through the valley of grief and despair or who are now experiencing that difficult situation, George's vision and the unconditional love that he received is meant to give us all hope when hope seems lost.

FLOATING ANGELS

AUTHOR'S NOTE: What is striking to me, as the author of this book, is how many people are visited by angels during the darkest part of their lives. I have received dozens and dozens of emails from people who never had an angelic intervention until they went through the loss of a spouse, child, or parent.

One would suppose, then, that God in his wisdom truly does understand how much we need hope, encouragement, and love at these times. Perhaps it is a divine thing that we do to give all of our love to another human being, all the while knowing that they could be taken from us at any given moment. To lose your loved one to death is often nearly unbearable. It takes more than just time when grieving to get to the other side of our pain. Many is the time that we've heard of someone who lost a spouse or child and, decades later, was still caught in a web of despair.

That is why it is so important for me to share with you, the reader, these wonderful stories of angelic intervention that bring hope.

I want to thank Jim Snyder for sharing his beautiful vision with us.

JIM'S WIFE PASSED AWAY FROM CANCER IN 2003. HE WAS incredibly distraught and grief stricken.

One night, he was praying to God to give him a sign to let him know that everything was going to be all right. He needed to know that his wife was happy and at peace, but he also needed to know that he would be given the grace and strength that would allow him to carry on with his own life.

The days moved into each other slowly, and still Jim did not receive his sign.

A little over a week later, Jim was lying in bed, fully awake.

Though his eyes were closed and he was trying to go to sleep, there is no doubt that Jim was completely awake.

Suddenly, a very strange feeling overwhelmed him. He opened his eyes, and hovering over his bed was an angel. All he saw of the angel was the upper torso and head. He did not see the full body. However, the angel did have wings. Around the face of the angel was a billowy circle of white clouds that seemed to be constantly churning. Everything in the vision was a brilliant white color, and the aura filled the room.

There was no music, sound, crackling, popping, or voices associated with the vision. It was perfectly silent.

The angel moved across the ceiling from left to right. The only communication that Jim received from the angel was a gentle smile.

The angel continued staring and smiling at him. Jim did not receive any messages, nor was there any verbal communication between the two of them.

The vision lasted about ten seconds and then slowly faded away. Jim was so awestruck that he couldn't move. After the image disappeared, all he could do was lie on the bed for several more minutes. He reports that he was filled with the most peaceful feeling he had ever experienced.

Several days after the vision came to him, Jim was alone and reading his Bible. He came across the following passage in Luke 22:43, which read, "And there appeared an angel unto him from heaven, strengthening him."

It was as if the angels were telling Jim, "If you didn't get the message from the pretty vision we sent you, here it is in writing."

From that day forward, Jim states that he was able to finally come to terms with his grief and the loss of his dear wife to cancer. He turned a new corner. Life became bearable once again. In the months that followed, his life took an even more positive turn.

The following year Jim met a wonderful lady and fell in love. He states that she is truly his soulmate. A year after they met, they were married in April of 2005.

In Jim's correspondence to me, he stated, "This incident had such an impact on my life I just wanted to share it in hopes of helping others who may be going through a hard time in their life."

Jim's story, like many others in this book, has brought tears to my eyes. How incredibly loving our God is to give us the angels to help us through the rough times and to bring a new love into our lives so that we can live every day in our fully human and divine capacity.

FIVE FRIENDLY ANGELS

AUTHOR'S NOTE: In the hundreds and hundreds of emails and letters I have received, there are many stories that are not all that long or involved and in which the recipient of the angelic visitation is shown only a glimpse of an angel or given only a short message. Although these experiences are brief, they are valuable to us because they are the kind of "divine nudge" that will help all of us to understand that angels are with us at all times. It appears, however, that angels reveal themselves at times of great stress, unhappiness, or chaos, or during life-and-death situations. Many readers have asked me why they haven't seen an angel, especially since they believe in them, have prayed for a "sighting," and truly have needed one. My answer is, "I don't know, really." My other answer is that most of us are angelically connected in our dreams, but we either dismiss these encounters as nonsense or we simply don't remember them. Sometimes we try to forget them. Other times, I think we are visited in broad daylight, but we don't see that person as an "angel" because they may not have wings. Also, there are times when we might see a shadow of a human figure out of the corner of our eye. Was that an angel? Possibly. My mother used to tell me that it was my eyes playing tricks on me. Also possible. However, if that fleeting shadow at the far end of the room forced me to be more careful that day, or perhaps I remembered someone I needed to contact who might need me, then I believe that was an angelic visitation.

Angel watching takes a lot of effort and consciousness on our part to constantly be aware.

The following three angelic glimpses were sent to me from Todd Walker.

FOUR YEARS AGO TODD WAS NOT ONLY GRIEVING OVER the loss of his grandfather, whom he loved very much, but it was also a time of deep loneliness. Though he had family around him, he had no love in his life and thus, felt empty. Todd's depression had spiraled down to that pit that a great many of us have experienced, although when one is going through it, we do feel utterly alone and abandoned.

Todd was lying in his bed, not asleep but awake and crying. Suddenly, he felt what he thought was a brush of the wind. However, the door and window were closed. There was no "wind" in his room. Then, he felt an electrical touch, a zing, on his hand. It seemed to have breached across the air and landed on his hand.

Incredibly, he realized it wasn't an electrical shock at all, but the touch of a real hand over his. The invisible "hand" rested on his hand for over ten seconds. There was no mistaking the pressure of the feeling, the weight of the hand. Todd knew at that moment that his grandfather was with him. For the first time in months, Todd felt loved again and filled with hope. From that moment, Todd's depression lifted completely.

In March 2006, Todd was tossing and turning trying to sleep. He gave up, opened his eyes, and just stared at the wall of his bedroom.

Without warning, five angels appeared right in front of his face. They swirled around the area in front of him. They appeared oddly small, as if Todd were looking at someone through binoculars who was two miles away.

In a few moments, all five angels moved away from their position in front of him and began swirling around his head. Now they appeared life-sized.

They had no messages to give him, leaving Todd to surmise that they wanted only to let him know that they existed and were with him.

At the same time in March 2006, a week or so after this apparition, Todd's niece told him that she had experienced a very explicit dream about heaven. She wanted to see her grandparents and her great-grandparents. When she arrived in heaven, she saw all the family members she had prayed to see. They were standing next to Jesus and smiled at her.

Satisfied that her grandparents were well and happy, she began to look around and take in her surroundings. She looked down and noticed that she was standing on flowers. However, these were very unusual flowers in that they were so bright that she wondered if they hadn't been painted. They were not like any colors she had seen on earth. Everywhere she looked she saw beauty beyond her imagination.

When she left and came back to earth, she shared her story with Todd. Within one week they had both experienced a visit from the angels.

MARY, MY GUARDIAN AND GUIDE

AUTHOR'S NOTE: This story is from Jerry Smith of Dayton, Ohio. In this book is a story from Claire Papin, who has also been visited by Mary, the Mother of Jesus. What is interesting to note in both these stories is that both Jerry and Claire, who live a thousand miles apart and have never met, were visited by Mother Mary, and neither is Catholic or was raised Catholic.

JERRY'S EXPERIENCE OCCURRED APPROXIMATELY A YEAR ago, when Jerry and his wife of thirty years were experiencing some very difficult, truly trying times. In fact, the financial situation was so perilous that Jerry lost his business after ten years of planning, dreaming, and a lot of hard work.

At the same time, Jerry suffered from life-threatening illnesses including heart failure, diabetes, and a ruptured appendix that required emergency surgery.

As always seemed to be the case, just when things couldn't get worse, they did. Jerry's adult children were going through difficulties that were potentially quite dangerous to the entire family.

The business closing led Jerry into bankruptcy, and they lost their home of many years, which took an emotional toll on everyone. Now they were forced to pack up all their belongings and find a new place to live. As bad luck would have it, Jerry's wife lost her job at the same time.

Depression, disappointment, and discouragement enveloped the entire family like a shroud. It was a wonder any of them could wake up in the morning and continue plodding through another day. But they did.

One particular morning, Jerry awoke about six thirty. Before he opened his eyes, he distinctly heard a soft but clearly audible mature woman's voice speaking. He knew it was not his wife's voice. At first, he thought it was his daughter's voice, who was living with them at the time, talking to his wife. But then he realized that he did not hear an exchange from his wife and this soft voice was not that of his daughter.

Jerry was fully awake now and opened his eyes.

He saw that his wife was sitting up on the edge of the bed, rubbing her face, putting on her slippers, and generally getting her thoughts together as she awakened to the new day.

Then Jerry saw a shape kneeling in front of his wife. This form was responsible for the soft voice he was hearing. Peering closely at the form, he saw that it was a woman, and she wore robes and a veil or shawl over her head.

He was instantly struck by the thought that this woman was Mother Mary, only because she resembled the statues and art work in which Mother Mary is often depicted. However, the figure never spoke her name or gave any reference to her identity.

Jerry's wife in the meantime was still sitting on the edge of the bed in the dark, completely unaware of anything that was happening.

Jerry continued to look at the figure, and as he did, it was as if she sensed that he could see her. Then the words or prayers that she was saying suddenly stopped. That soft voice just ceased.

Then slowly, her form faded. She was gone.

It was as if Jerry had "caught" her. He was struck with the notion that she was thinking to herself, "Oops! I've been caught! I have to go!"

Jerry continued to stare blankly at the space that had only moments ago been filled by a heavenly being. He was at once filled with a profound sense of peace and calm. He realized that what he had just experienced was beyond awesome.

Because the notion of Mother Mary popped so suddenly into Jerry's head and because she is not a person or religious figure that he thinks about very often, if at all, I believe that she might have been trying to tell him who she was.

Jerry also believes that it is likely that he "surprised" this being by seeing her and that perhaps the encounter might have been an accident.

There are those who would say, "There are no accidents with God." There are also those who would say Jerry and his family deserved a miracle. And they got one.

ADDENDUM: This is a short snippet of a story, but interesting, and I have decided to include it as well.

Jerry has an aunt who believes that she saw her guardian angel in much the same fashion that Jerry witnessed the woman's figure kneeling next to his wife. Several years ago, Jerry's aunt stated that she saw the shape of a man's arm leaving her room one day.

Such a "fleeing angel" sighting is easy to explain away for most of us, but the real test is the following. Just after Jerry's aunt saw the man's arm, she was flooded with a sense of peace and well-being.

As I have stated throughout this book, the difference between imagination and real encounters with the divine is twofold. First, once you have such an experience, it seems very, very real, and you never forget it. Second, there is always a strong sense of either being loved unconditionally or being at peace such as you have not known before.

Both Jerry's aunt and Jerry experienced these important criteria with their angel encounters.

JESUS IN THE MORNING

AUTHOR'S NOTE: This story was sent to me just recently, but this lady does not want me to use her real name. I will call her Emma. Whether sent to me anonymously or not, the fact of the matter is that this story is very real and it DID happen.

I think that one of the reasons the author or "experiencer" wants to remain unnamed is that she admits to not "being particularly religious." However, she states that she has "always felt a connection with Jesus."

She says further, "As I said, I am not a Christian, nor have I ever had a vision like this before. I just wanted to share it with you because it had some similarities to your experience of Christ."

When I receive stories like this, I am truly taken aback. How interesting it is to me that with all the Christians I know who are praying and begging Jesus to show up, literally, in their lives, he chooses to appear to someone who pointedly admits they are not Christian. Such incidents are again a reminder that God, in all his forms and with all his messengers and forms of messaging, will meet our needs—always.

EMMA'S NIGHT HAD BEEN FILLED WITH VERY FRIGHTEN-ing dreams. It was early in the morning when she began to awaken. She wasn't asleep because this was not a dream. However, she admits that she was not fully awake either. She was "between" sleep and wakefulness.

Because the dreams had truly been scary, she called on Jesus to protect her.

To her surprise, a shape appeared outside her bedroom door. "No. No. No!" she said.

At the very moment she saw the shape, she knew instinctively that the shape had not come to harm her. She felt in her heart and mind that it was Jesus, but she also believed she was not really ready to see him. Everything about that moment was real to Emma. She knew she was not living in a dream.

She sat upright.

Jesus walked into the room despite her protest. He stood right in front of her. She looked at his face, but it was filled with light. The light didn't hurt, but it prevented her from being able to make out his exact features. He was very tall and large boned and wore blue robes.

"I want you to lie back down, Emma."

Emma watched as he held out his hands to her.

Emma was so stunned and so shocked at his very presence that she couldn't move. She just sat there staring at him.

Finally, he kneeled down next to her and whispered in her ear, "I am the One that stands behind you all the time."

Emma was flooded with a sense of unconditional love and protection. She felt his words ring true in her heart and soul.

Then he was gone.

But the profound sense of the incredulity of the incident did not leave Emma.

Later that day, she told one of her close friends about the incident, and as she began to speak, Emma's eyes swam with tears. Her words caught in her throat, burning themselves into her memory. She began sobbing uncontrollably as she remembered the unconditional love she had felt from Jesus.

"It was unbelievable," Emma finally managed to tell her friend. "It was as if all this love in the universe was directed just at me. I felt that he has the gift of making each and every one of us feel particularly loved, as if he is there for you and you alone."

Emma knew not only that her experience was rare but also that she would never forget it.

It is her gift to others to share this story with us.

PRAYER FOR LIFE

AUTHOR'S NOTE: This story from Sandy Teslow of Sioux Falls, Iowa, is yet another remarkable peek into the divine dimension that exists alongside our earth plane.

WHEN I WAS SEVENTEEN AND A SENIOR IN HIGH school, our Sunday School teacher, who was pastor of our Presbyterian church, suggested during a discussion about prayer that rather than just saying things like, "God, bless my family," it might be more appropriate to pray for each person by name. This would make our prayers much more personal, and if we knew a specific area of need, we could speak to that.

So, I did.

My prayer was very long, I became very relaxed and feared I would go to sleep before I'd prayed for every single person. As I was nearing the end, I became aware that I had lost feeling in my feet. I moved them a bit, didn't feel them, and then noticed that this lack of feeling was moving up my legs in a very methodical and even manner. As it had moved to the trunk of my body and was completely consuming me, I asked God if I was dying, because if I was, I was ready to do so.

A voice in my ear said, "No, my child, you aren't dying."

I then let him know that I definitely did not understand what was happening.

At this point, my room was filled with a bright, though soft, white light. It started at the edge of the foot of my bed and extended to the rest of the room from that point, wall to wall.

Within the light stood Jesus. His garment was a brilliant white.

I believe that our physical eyes would not be able to gaze upon it. It would be the same as looking directly at the sun.

He smiled at me, even showed me his hands, both sides, and I saw the scars from the wounds. I think he did this just to prove to me who he was and that I was safe.

He affirmed that I was not dying. "My child, it is not your time. I have a job for you to do."

"What kind of job?" I asked.

"You will know in due time, my child. You will know in due time."

As I gazed at his beautiful face, I tried to memorize it so I could describe him.

I must have blinked or closed my eyes because when I looked at him again, I saw the robe and the figure. This time, as I looked at his face, I saw no face. Rather, I saw what appeared to be space—yes, deep space where his face was.

I guess at that point, I fell asleep.

The next morning I realized something wonderfully unusual had happened to me, but I couldn't remember anything. I pondered this all day at school to no avail. As I was walking home, I guess I was about a block or two away, that's when I remembered.

I literally ran all the way home to tell my mom. Mother was very interested in my story. First of all, she was most pleased and took it in stride. She told me that while she was pregnant with each of us children, she prayed for us, and every day after our birth. She saw my experience as part of her prayers being answered. She considered this experience a blessing.

In our discussion, she suggested that I be very careful if I ever shared this story with anyone. In fact, she felt it would be best if I didn't tell the story, because of what other people would think and how they would react.

The next Sunday, I was burning to tell somebody about my experience. So, I chose the youth leader. She was a young woman who was studying for the ministry. Much to my amazement, her reaction was exactly as Mother had feared. She didn't take to it kindly at all. With a scowl on her face and ice in her voice, she looked me directly in the eye and said, "That's a dream! And you had better forget it!"

I never told our pastor because I was afraid of the response I'd get from him as well.

My experience happened to me in 1954. It wasn't until the 1960s that I heard that voice again. It said, "It's your spiritual life that's missing."

After that revelation, I joined a Bible study group, and in January of 1970, I turned my life over to Jesus.

At this point in my life, I still don't know what "job" Jesus wanted me to do. I've done lots of things, and I can only hope I have served him to this point. I liken my experience to being led, by him, through different rooms in a museum where one can look at all sorts of things and study things that are of interest, but I was led through it. I couldn't live, or settle, in any one of those rooms. I still pray for the help of the angels to guide me.

I would love to hear that "definitive" voice again. My experience was wondrous, and I have been blessed all my life to have experienced it at such a young age. I will never forget it. Even if I can't remember exactly what Jesus's face looked like, I will always remember the peace and love I felt when he appeared to me.

SECTION EIGHT

Angel Warnings in Dreams

ANGEL WARNINGS
IN DREAMS

THE MOST LIKELY TIME THAT MOST OF US WILL SEE AN angel is in our dreams. Our dream state appears to be a virtual connection to our spiritual self and the spiritual dimension.

These are the dreams that we never forget. The warnings can be lifesaving at times, but many times the warnings are about our health or our loved ones. Perhaps the angel wants us to pay particular attention to a child who may be about to meet some kind of dangerous situation or a particularly difficult time with his or her peers.

In my own family, our experience with dreams in which there are warnings of one kind or another are plentiful. Personally, I expect to be given divine warnings on a permanent basis for the rest of my life. I wouldn't have gotten this far or lived this long if I had not been paying attention to the messages I've received from an angel or departed loved one.

If you do experience this kind of dream, do yourself a favor and write it down in a log book or journal as soon as you wake up. Jot down as much as you can possibly remember. Even nonsensical things at your awakening may prove to make perfect sense later. Nothing should be overlooked.

We all need to pay attention to our dreams more than we do for many reasons. They are illuminations into our own psyches and help us to understand ourselves and the situations we encounter in our lives.

The angels think your dreams are important. Why shouldn't you?

Mary Paine's Prophetic Dream

I HAVE ALWAYS HAD SOME VERY VIVID DREAMS, AS DID MY mother. Some of our dreams have been prophetic. Most of these dreams have been about things that are soon to happen in our lives rather than events that happen to friends or strangers.

I have had several dreams that have warned me about a loved one dying. One of the most vivid of these dreams occurred in January 1999. In the dream, I heard a big booming male voice that I have since come to call "the voice of God." I know it probably wasn't God, but rather an angel. That night the voice told me, "You need to know that Ladd is going to die, but you will be just fine."

At the time, I thought that my dream was about my father, who is named Dwight Ladd. I woke up hysterical. I kept telling my husband that this can't be! It would never be all right! I would never be fine if my father died. I was very close to my father and loved him dearly. Just the thought of his being ill, much less dying, was nearly more than I could take. No matter how much my husband consoled me, for weeks all I could hear in my head was that booming "voice of God."

About three months later, I had just about forced myself not to think about the awful prediction by the voice, when my oldest brother, whom I called Laddie, died suddenly of congestive heart failure. He was only fifty-two years old. Now my "dream" made perfect, but sorrowful, sense. In addition, I realized that this voice that comes to me is a warning messenger's voice and that I should trust in what it tells me. I may not have actually seen an angel, but I believe I have certainly heard one.

BEARS AND ANGELS—OH, MY!

AUTHOR'S NOTE: This story was submitted by Helen Zapata of Phoenix, Arizona.

IN THE LATE 1970S, HELEN AND HER THEN-HUSBAND, Mark, used to do a lot of walking, hiking, and bicycling. They did not own a car, but it didn't bother them a bit. They loved the outdoors, and the more they could be in it, the happier they were.

With great anticipation, they planned a trip to Yosemite National Park to go backpacking. Their plans called for taking a bus to get there, and then they figured they would simply head off into the wilderness and enjoying nature. Prior to the trip, Helen read everything she could on Yosemite Park, hoping to get a real layout of the land in her head before their arrival.

It was from her reading that she learned how important it was to take the appropriate measures while camping so that the bears would not bother them. This warning caused her a great deal of distress. BEARS? The terror of childhood nightmares filled her thoughts. Not once had she ever thought that they would encounter an actual live bear. Bears were something you saw in movies and documentaries, not in real life. Or so she thought.

The weeks passed, and even though her concern escalated, it was time for them to leave.

The drive from Laguna Beach to Yosemite was fantastic. Helen and her husband truly enjoyed all the sights they saw. They arrived at the park just after dark and found that the campground on the valley floor was completely full. Their plan had been to spend just one night there and then to hike up into the back country. It had never occurred to Helen or her husband that they would need to make a reservation simply to roll out a sleeping bag for the night.

Not knowing what to do, they wandered around in the pitch black night trying to find a place to sleep. Understandably, they were both exhausted after the very long bus ride. They finally found a patch of ground away from the crowd and plunked down their sleeping bags. Within minutes they were both asleep.

Helen was sound asleep when she heard a booming voice wake her up. It was a male's voice, and he spoke very clearly. She knew that the voice was not from outside of her head but inside of her head. This was no still small voice like the voice of our sub-consciousness. To Helen it was as real as any normal person speaking—except that it was inside her. And it was a man's voice.

The voice said, "Be careful. Remember the bear can see you."

Helen was instantly and fully awake. She felt no fear whatsoever. She kept very still, with her eyes closed, and she waited.

In the next few moments, she felt the ground underneath her vibrating as something very large silently approached her. She laid stock still. A very large head pushed itself underneath her sleeping bag, directly under her head, and pushed her head around and kept sniffing the area. She kept her body as still as possible, trying not even to breathe.

Again the animal continued to move her head around. She felt his warm breath on her face and the tickle of his fur. She felt the tickle of his fur as he sniffed at her head.

Finally, after several long moments, the animal withdrew. Helen felt the ground vibrating as the large animal walked down the length of her left side and then continued on its way.

As unbelievable as this encounter was, Helen felt no fear whatsoever. She was filled with calm. She was so calm, in fact, that after the animal left, she simply went back to sleep.

The next morning, Helen told her husband about the incident. But even as she was telling it, the whole thing felt like an afterthought to her. Again she was amazed at how calm she had been and still was. Perhaps it was because of her inner peace about the situation that her husband did not believe her. He claimed the animal could have been no more than a raccoon or a dog.

This reasoning made no sense to Helen whatsoever. For one thing, a dog or a raccoon does not make the earth vibrate when it walks around. Second, she knew exactly what the voice had told her. She had been warned explicitly to not be afraid of the bear.

"Why would the voice tell me to be careful and to remember that the bear can see me? Clearly, it told me that the animal was a bear!"

During the rest of the backpacking trip, Helen remained completely calm. She had none of the fear that she'd had during the weeks prior to their trip.

Helen believes today that God sent her this particular experience so that she would always know and remember that her life was safely in his hands. She had nothing to worry about—ever.

SECTION NINE

Divine Nudges

DIVINE NUDGES

DIVINE NUDGES ARE NOT SIMPLY A GENTLE REMINDER that you need to try a little harder to be a bit kinder to your friend or family member. To be honest, if only we all did precisely that much every day of our lives all day long, we just might stop war and domestic violence, and empty our prisons. Divine nudges in our stories are divine "get a clue" situations that alter our thinking and affect our lives, our career paths, and our relationships for the good.

These moments may be what many would consider traumatic times: the sudden loss of employment, a divorce or romantic breakup, sudden death of a partner, death of a best friend, unexpected job relocation, a very serious health issue, or the tragic loss of a dwelling due to fire, flood, earthquake, hurricane, or tsunami.

For over two decades I have worked with, spoken out for, and supported in my own way the victims of domestic violence. For these women and their abused children, escaping their violent husbands or boyfriends is incredibly traumatic. As horrific as their lives are inside the walls of abuse, it is their comfort zone. Most women stay in these marriages and relationships for financial security or because their religion teaches they cannot divorce. For some, it is family pressure that makes them stay. They are told that the embarrassment of a divorce is greater than the physical violence or verbal threats to the abuse victim. In far too many instances, the woman fears that her husband will murder her or the children if she leaves. Too many times, these threats are real.

When an abused woman finally finds the courage to escape her abuser, the alteration in her life requires substantial angelic intervention. It may happen on the day when her husband has threatened physical violence and finally hits her.

She is bruised and bleeding, but she leaves him shortly thereafter. For years she has tolerated verbal abuse. She has been "put down" in public. Most abusers cut their victims' ability to communicate with their family or friends. Abusers are possessive and obsessive. They demand to be made the center of the universe. It is "their way or the highway." To maintain control, abusers must "up the ante" over a period of years until the point comes when they reach their boiling point and physical violence becomes their next step.

Many times circumstances occur that cause the abuser to explode that, to the victims, seem completely out of their control. This explosion can be quite violent. However, this eruption is the very moment of the divine nudge. The victim must finally make a decision on her own to leave. She can't go back anymore. She can't take it anymore, and her only option is to leave.

Once she is out on her own, she begins to think of her life with all new rules, parameters, and options.

She has begun to live her life for herself by her rules.

The victim then realizes that she has been "nudged" from a negative plane of existence to a much higher plane of love and abundance. She must realize she can "live without him" and his money. Most important, she must believe in herself enough to face the world alone.

This woman's life and the lives of her children, if she has any, have been "nudged" into a divine sphere.

A divine nudge can occur when a total stranger enters your life for only a brief moment or a single day and shows you the tools of your talent or a destiny that perhaps you didn't even know you had or which has been lying dormant for years.

In our stories here from Peg Melnick and Gail Mitchell, both women believed in prayer and relied on prayer to give their lives a divine nudge.

They asked, and they received.

Prayer works.

REAL ESTATE ANGEL

DIVORCE IS DIFFICULT FOR ANYONE TO ENDURE. FOR many, the emotional pain is equivalent to the grief one experiences when a loved one has died. In addition to the grief, there are feelings of betrayal and oftentimes the loss of a best friend.

For most women, divorce also means significantly reduced financial circumstances.

When Gail Mitchell divorced due to her situation, she was forced to move into a crummy apartment, half of which was built into a basement. The space was rampant with spiders and terrible mold that not only gave Gail headaches but also caused her thirteen-year-old daughter to have many allergies.

Gail was determined to create a better home for herself and her child. She saved her money, cashed in some of her retirement, and prepared to buy a brand new house.

She went to her financial services company to take ten thousand dollars out of her retirement fund. The officer filled out the paperwork. Gail then had it notarized and gave it back. The officer then placed the paperwork, along with that of several other clients, put it in a FedEx envelope, and placed it in the FedEx box outside their offices.

Gail waited and waited for word from the company but finally heard that someone had stolen the package from the FedEx box! The company was working their way down the list of all the people who'd had paperwork stolen, and she appeared to be the last one.

A week later, one of Gail's coworkers had the idea that maybe, just maybe, it might have been kids who stole the FedEx packages. She called the police with her idea. The police actually thought it was a good idea and went looking in the woods behind the building.

Unbelievably, the package was found in the snow, soggy but intact.

At this point, Gail could not imagine what was going on in her life.

It took a lot of doing on her part and a lot of legwork, but she finally was approved for a bank loan. She knew that she was going to have to continue to make many sacrifices in order to afford the house, but she was willing to do it because she wanted a good environment for her daughter.

A week or so after being approved for the loan, the price of the house escalated before Gail could put in an offer. This caused the bank to rerun her credit check. In that very short period of time, a bad credit report appeared on Gail's file. Apparently, her ex-husband had refused to pay for a piece of furniture that he had previously promised to pay. He still owned the furniture, and by all rights, he was responsible for the debt.

In order to get the bad mark off her credit report, Gail was forced to pay the furniture off.

In the ensuing days, nothing that Gail did seemed to change her bad credit rating. After she had paid the furniture off, the company sent a letter stating that the account was no longer due. However, they sent it to the wrong address. The credit company did not receive the letter. Gail followed up with more letters and more inquiries, but it all went wrong.

Nothing Gail did seemed to fix her credit rating enough for the bank to give her the loan she needed.

She went to the bank and explained to them that she would even put up another 10,000 dollars for the down payment in order to be able to procure this dream house of hers. However, the bank refused. She thought she was completely out of options.

Gail prayed. She prayed more.

In January 2006, the government forced all the credit card companies to charge customers more on their monthly payment to pay off the principal faster. This new law forced Gail to double her credit card payments. Now she knew she was never going to get her house. If she had bought her house, she realized at this point that she never would have been able to keep it because her credit card payments had increased so substantially. Gail then took the 10,000 dollars that she had amassed and used it to pay off all of her credit cards.

She started looking for a new apartment because she thought it was all she could afford.

Out of the blue, she came upon an ad for a rental house that was open, airy, and built on the side of a mountain, and had everything brand new, including all the appliances, floors, doors, and carpet. It was everything that she had ever dreamed of and more.

Gail knows today that whenever she gets her head against that immovable object, that very sturdy brick wall that we all meet sooner or later, just around the next corner is going to be that divine intervention that we are all looking for.

MARVIN THE "NEW YEAR'S DAY MIRACLE"

AUTHOR'S NOTE: This story was sent to me by Peg Melnik. I kept the story in her words in order to keep the emotion and wonder of her voice as strong as possible.

T HE DOCTORS AND PARAMEDICS AT THORNTON HOSPI-
tal at the University of California, San Diego, coined Marvin the "New Year's Day Miracle" because the ninety-one-year-old defied medical logic and survived, completely unscathed, from a choking episode that left him unconscious for about five minutes.

I witnessed Marvin's miracle firsthand. Marvin is like a father to me, and we were at his house on the afternoon of New Year's Eve 2005, when the choking incident happened.

Marvin tried to swallow two large extra strength Tylenols for chronic neck pain, but they lodged in his throat, and he choked. My mother and daughter called 911 while I stayed with Marvin.

I knew I wasn't strong enough to lift Marvin up and do the Heimlich maneuver, but I was determined to help him. Marvin was beginning to turn purple because he couldn't breathe. He couldn't even gasp for air, and he looked at me with vulnerable, frantic, pleading eyes. I was distraught, feeling utterly helpless, but then I realized I could help Marvin.

I remembered reading a story in the book *Angel Watch* by Catherine Lanigan about a faith healer who helped Catherine's brother overcome a serious illness with prayer.

I began to pray with everything I had in me for this man I love so dearly. I told God to deliver Marvin—to move the pills lodged in his throat so he could breathe in air. I told God that Marvin was needed here and that we all loved him so much. I cried and I prayed.

And then I was amazed by what happened.

Exactly what I prayed for happened. Marvin, who was now unconscious, regained his color, and with his mouth open, he began to breathe in air ever so slightly. I kept watching his mouth to make sure I wasn't imagining it.

About five minutes later, the paramedics arrived. As they worked on Marvin, who lay unconscious, I put my hands on his chest and put Reiki energy into him while I prayed some more.

I'm a Reiki practitioner, and Reiki is an ancient Japanese method of hands-on healing. It's based on the belief that love from the universe heals people.

The paramedics didn't seem to notice or care what I was doing, as they continued to work on Marvin. During their attempt to place a laryngoscope, Marvin awoke from his unconsciousness.

The paramedics took Marvin to the hospital, and during the ride, Marvin made jokes and behaved like his usual self, according to my mother, who rode with him in the ambulance.

Once Marvin was at the hospital, he was given a series of tests, including an EKG that was unchanged from a prior test. Marvin passed all the tests with flying colors, including a current events quiz doctors give to make sure a patient hasn't lost any memory.

Marvin's doctor at the hospital told me that he was the talk of the emergency room medical staff. She and the others couldn't believe a ninety-one-year old could come out of a choking episode like this completely unscathed.

Meanwhile one of the paramedics told my mother, "I've been in this business for seventeen years, and I've never seen an outcome like this."

Marvin's experience gives me confidence. If someone is in distress, you don't have to feel helpless. I have a powerful resource: prayer.

So do you.

A NOTE FROM THE AUTHOR

Dear Reader,

I hope that you found these stories of value in your life and that you now realize that angels have been visiting you quite regularly. If you have a story you would like to share for the next book on angels that I'm writing, please email it to cathlanigan@aol.com. You can also contact me on Facebook. Please include your contact information, including a phone number, so that I can call you and discuss your story and its presentation.

The angels and I are grateful for your participation. Keeping an open mind is the first step in keeping your angel watch. Sharing angelic sightings is a courageous act and will benefit so many others who are still looking for answers and comfort in their times of grief, crisis, and pain.

God Bless You All,

Catherine Lanigan

ABOUT THE AUTHOR

CATHERINE LANIGAN IS THE BESTSELLING AUTHOR OF nearly thirty-five published titles, both fiction and nonfiction, including the novelizations of *Romancing the Stone* and *The Jewel of the Nile*. She has contributed stories in over half a dozen anthologies, including *Chicken Soup for the Soul: Living your Dream*, *Chicken Soup for the Writer's Soul*, *Chocolate for a Woman's Heart*, and *Chocolate for a Woman's Spirit*. Ms. Lanigan's novels have been translated into over a dozen languages, including German, French, Italian, Spanish, Russian, Portuguese, Chinese, and Japanese. Her novels are also available on audiocassette and CD and can be purchased as e-books on Amazon.com and BarnesandNoble.com.

Several of her titles have been chosen for the Literary Guild and Doubleday Book Clubs. Her Vietnam War–based novel, *The Christmas Star*, won the Gold Medal Award Top Pick from

Romantic Times Magazine, the Book of the Year Romance Gold Award from *ForeWord Magazine,* and Book of the Year—Romance from Readers Preference. *Divine Nudges: Tales of Angelic Intervention* and the second in Lanigan's *Angel Watch* series of books was published by HCI. Allworth Press released Lanigan's "how-to" book on writing: *Writing the Great American Romance Novel.* Lanigan recently completed "notMYkid," a nonfiction work regarding teen addictions, which was commissioned by the notMYkid foundation. In addition, Ms. Lanigan is working on a three-book series of young adult adventure novels, *The Adventures of Lillie and Zane: The Golden Flute* to be published by Cedar Fort, Inc.

Ms. Lanigan is a frequent speaker at literary functions and book conventions and inspires audiences with her real stories of angelic intervention from her Angel Tales series. She is an outspoken advocate against domestic violence and abuse and was honored by The National Domestic Violence Hotline in Washington, DC. She has been a guest on numerous radio programs including *Coast to Coast* and on television interview and talk show programs such as *Montel.* Catherine's email is cathlanigan@aol.com.